The Cowboy's Daughter

The Cowboy's Daughter

A Three Sisters Ranch Romance

Jamie K. Schmidt

TULE
PUBLISHING

Chapter One

KELLY SULLIVAN KNEW she was nitpicking about what filter to use for the engagement photo she was processing. The bride wouldn't be able to tell the difference between the gradients, but fussing over the nearly perfect picture kept Kelly from thinking about the message her father had left on her phone.

Come home one last time. We're selling the ranch. We can't keep up with the bills.

It was amazing that he'd even tried to call her. Usually, he just had her mom do it. And for him to admit a failing? Well, that worried her. Rule number one: Frank Sullivan was never wrong. And if he ever was? See rule number one.

Kelly couldn't stop herself from analyzing his message, looking for hidden meanings in his tone and the things he didn't say. It was a self-defense mechanism she'd used ever since he tossed her out on her pregnant ass because she wouldn't tell him who the father of her baby was. While that was five years ago, their tentative truce was fraught with emotions neither one of them wanted to deal with. The tightrope they walked could snap, and one or the other of them could say or do something that couldn't be repaired.

"We can't keep up with the bills" was a weakness. And the only thing her father loathed more than weakness, was giving up.

"We're selling the ranch." Where would they go? Both her mother and her father had lived in Last Stand, Texas all their lives. Kelly couldn't imagine them wanting to live anywhere else.

"Come home one last time." She was already home. The Three Sisters Ranch ceased to become her home when he'd thrown her out. They hadn't spoken for two years after that. Home wasn't a vast five-thousand-acre ranch with dusty cows and hauntingly beautiful sunsets. It was an apartment in a thriving city, where people didn't know your business and couldn't care less if you were a single mother, or had had a child out of wedlock.

Her five-year-old daughter, Alissa went to preschool here, had friends here. Kelly stayed away from Last Stand, Texas, to avoid the unwed mother gaze her father would bestow on her every day of her life. And even after his heart attack, when they'd had a grudging reconciliation, she'd still only been back for holidays and special occasions. But even though Kelly tried to avoid how she felt about the place and the memories it conjured up, the truth couldn't be ignored. The Three Sisters Ranch was still a part of her. It was a part of them all. And even though she could hail a cab like a native New Yorker, one never truly left Last Stand.

Her sisters were equally shocked by their messages. He must have timed it so he could talk to all of their answering machines instead of them. Janice was scrambling to rearrange her schedule. Emily was on her way back from Ethiopia, where she'd been living once her term in the Peace Corps had expired. They had FaceTimed with their mom, though, and while they all had different ideas on how to save the ranch, the one thing they could all agree on was they were going to try their damned best not to sell.

Their mother, Sarah, had been glad that her daughters were coming home and that they were willing to try and find ways to make the ranch profitable again. No word from her father, though, after the original message, which was typical. Frank Sullivan was like a grenade. He came in and exploded everywhere and then disappeared, leaving everyone to pick up the shattered pieces.

"When's your flight?" her aunt Candace said, bringing Kelly a cup of coffee and placing it on her desk. Candace had left Texas as soon as she graduated high school and had lived in Manhattan ever since. She was a sought-after wedding planner, and had taken Kelly in when she could no longer bear the looks of shame her parents hadn't tried to hide.

"I haven't booked it yet." Kelly moved on from the engagement photo to the school pictures she needed to get out to the parents this week. She'd been lucky enough to win the bid on the Academy of Arts Elementary School yearly portraits and she wanted to impress the heck out of them so she'd be invited back next year. Still, in the back of her mind, she was picturing the spring bluebonnet flowers that decorated the ranch with a royal blue so rich it uplifted your heart. There had to be schools in Texas that were looking for photographers.

"There's nothing you can do from here, that you can't do from there."

Blinking out of her daydreams, Kelly nodded. It was true. Have laptop, will travel. "I hate to drag Alissa out of summer school."

"It's pre-kindergarten. It's not like she's going to miss out on a whole lot. And doesn't that fancy-pants school encourage nontraditional learning? You can learn a lot on a cattle ranch."

"Especially if you listen to the hands. Talk about a vocabulary lesson I don't want my daughter repeating back to her city-slicker friends." Kelly grinned, playing up her Texas drawl for effect.

Candace sniffed. "Your parents need Alissa right now. She's the only good thing they have—aside from you three girls, of course."

"Nice catch," Kelly said.

Alissa was the glue that held her family together, and it was a fragile bond. When Kelly's daughter was born, her mother had called and tried to re-establish their relationship. Kelly had needed her mother, even though she hadn't stuck up for her when her father had thrown her out, and she gratefully took the opportunity to reconnect with her. But her father had remained stoically firm in his ultimatum...until a few years later, when he lay recovering in his hospital bed. Then, he demanded to meet his only grandchild. Her sisters had always made it a point to call every week to see how Kelly and Alissa were doing. Alissa was the best thing that had happened to Kelly, even if she had turned her life upside down. But babies were supposed to do that, right?

"I can also help my parents from right here," Kelly said, defiantly. "I don't have to uproot my life and my daughter's." There was that simmering resentment she still felt for them. It was hard to let go of it. The betrayal. She had waited for her mother, at least, to come to her senses and tell her father to stop being ridiculous. Of course, her six-months-pregnant daughter could stay. Of course, she didn't have to tell them who the father was until she was ready.

No.

Her mother had stood on the porch and let tears flow down her cheeks, unchecked. But she hadn't stood up for Kelly. Or Alissa.

"Your sisters are going. Emily is coming from another continent. You can't get on a three-hour flight?"

Kelly took a bracing sip of her coffee, feeling the burn of her aunt's logic. How could she explain, without feeling petty, that she was still hurt from something that should have been resolved long ago? Her parents had never apologized. Then again, they'd never brought up the subject again. And Kelly couldn't find any fault in how they treated Alissa. She was the apple of their eyes and they doted on her, even long distance.

Kelly had once been the apple of their eyes. Until one day, she wasn't.

"Just go down for a few weeks. Assess the situation. Talk with your sisters and spend time with them without the craziness of the holidays getting in the way."

The irony of the ranch being named after them was that none of the three sisters had stayed. Her father's temperament was partly to blame. He wasn't an easy man to live with. Frank Sullivan had high expectations and a low tolerance for anyone or anything that didn't measure up.

His temper and demanding ways aside, he could never see that his baby girls had grown up to become independent women, with their own high expectations and low tolerances—along with stubborn streaks that they'd inherited from him. To him, they were forever twelve, ten and eight, even fifteen years later.

Kelly had been the first to fly the coop, with the helpful shove from her father's ultimatum. Twenty-two and pregnant, she refused to tell anyone who the father of her child was. And that was because he hadn't acknowledged that Alissa was his. Kelly had refused to drag her family's name through the dirt, trying to get professional bull rider, Trent Campbell, to do the right thing.

When she had found out she was pregnant, it had been like all the air in the room had vanished. She had panicked. He had a huge tour scheduled and she was still finishing up her degree in business management. After their one-night stand, they had exchanged phone numbers and promised to keep in touch. But they hadn't. With her course work and his crazy hours, what started out as a daily text fest, dwindled to once a week, and then not at all. In the back of her mind, Kelly knew that she would see him again. He was sure to come back for next year's rodeo.

But three months later, Kelly had needed to text him to

call her. He never did. She'd left him a voice mail, which he'd never returned. She'd even tried to track him down through his manager.

"If he wants to be a father, have him call me. If he doesn't, I never want to hear from him again."

That's what she told Trent's manager, Billy King. And Trent never contacted her again.

His loss.

"What's the real reason you don't want to go back?" Candace asked.

Kelly shook her head to clear it of memories and saved the school portraits she was working on. They were fine. The parents would love them. And if they didn't, she was very handy with Photoshop. Sighing, Kelly stretched in her chair and looked out the window into the bustling city, thinking about how to answer her aunt. There were a lot of reasons Kelly didn't want to go back. She picked the one that was easiest to explain.

"I don't want to say goodbye. I know I don't go back very often, but the ranch was always there waiting for me. I suppose looking back, I should have seen that things needed to be repaired and painted. But I never thought they were in trouble financially."

"It wasn't your business to know." Candace sat down at her own desk and fired up her computer.

"I should have suspected after Dad's heart attack."

"At least they're doing the right thing and selling now, before the bank forecloses."

Kelly jumped up and began to pace around the small office. She and Alissa lived with Aunt Candace and Kelly worked out of the apartment. When they'd first moved in, the hardest thing to get used to was how cramped everything was in New York. The second hardest thing was all the noise. "What if they didn't have to sell the ranch?"

"Did you win Powerball when I wasn't looking?" her aunt asked dryly.

"Hear me out." Kelly took a big gulp of coffee for courage. "What if instead of going down for just a week or two for a visit, I can convince my dad to rent me some land to set up a portrait studio or photo gallery? I bet I could bring in a good amount of business."

"I'm so glad I wasn't drinking when you said that. I would have spurted coffee out of my nose. Your father? Allowing strangers on his land?"

Kelly waved her hand. "Yeah, I know. It's something I've always wanted to do and the rents here in the city are astronomical. But in Last Stand? I've got some money saved up. At least a few months' worth of rent." Of course, she was putting herself back into a position where her parents could toss her out again if they didn't like what she was doing. And this time, she had Alissa. But the desire for her own business warred with that little pessimistic voice in her head.

"Your father won't take your money," Candace dismissed.

"Not if I gave it to him. But if I told him that I wanted to start my own business? Establish myself in Last Stand." Kelly nodded. "He'd rent to me."

"Especially if it meant he'd see Alissa every day."

"There's that, too."

Kelly hadn't been thinking about much else since she got the message a few weeks ago. If she could start a business and help make the ranch profitable again—or at least get back on its feet, maybe she could redeem herself in her parents' eyes. Although a part of her wondered why she needed that affirmation. "We could start out with bridal and engagement photos."

"We?" Candace said, arching her eyebrow. "I don't know anyone in Texas anymore."

"Yes, but you know people who know people. I can put up a wedding pavilion and some other things like a gazebo and an archway. The pictures would be fantastic. Especially at sunset."

"All right, I'll play along. Let's say you can convince your father to allow strangers to tramp all over his property for pictures. And let's say you can get a bride or two to buy into the scenic views. How is this going to help save the ranch from foreclosure? Your yearly rent would be something, but I don't think it will be enough."

"Janice and Emily have ideas, as well."

Candace put her hand over her face. "Oh dear. I almost feel sorry for your poor parents."

"We've already run our ideas by Mom, and she's good with this. One last try to save the homestead before selling."

"So, what's the holdup? I figured you'd be racing to get there and get started."

"Well, it seems that our idea wasn't really unique. Mom had already asked around town if there was anyone who wanted to lease parts of the ranch, and the word went out far and wide. No one from Last Stand came forward, at least, not yet. But they have one person already on board. I don't know much about the deal. Mom was pretty vague, but they gave hunting rights to a game hunter. She mentioned he might take a few hunting tours through to try it out. He might also rent some land. It could get a little crowded."

Candace winced. "Emily isn't going to be happy about that."

"Yeah," Kelly said. Emily was a vegetarian and a complete mystery to her family, and most of Texas.

"I truly don't see why you can't have game hunters and your businesses on the ranch, as long as it's scheduled right, and you can keep out of Nate's way for the cattle drives."

That was her sister Janice's job. Nate Pierson had been her father's foreman forever and he'd always had a sweet spot for Janice. So if she could keep him happy, and Emily could keep her father happy or at least distracted, it could work.

"There's plenty of land to go around. That's the one thing they've got in abundance. I guess it's about time to start making it more productive," Candace said. She squinted at the calendar. "Isn't the Last Stand Rodeo next week? Fourth of July. Alissa will love that."

Yeah, about that.

"She's going to be a cute rodeo princess someday, just like her mother was."

Kelly hid a smile. It was easy to picture her sunshine girl in full regalia bouncing along on her horse. But that was still years away. Right now, Kelly had to get through the rest of

June and past the Last Stand Rodeo.

"Hey, Trent Campbell is going to be the master of ceremonies. Local boy comes home. Oh, your father must be over the moon about that. He was a huge fan before Trent's accident ended his career."

And that was the real reason she wasn't already on a plane.

"Hmm." Kelly hoped that sounded noncommittal enough. She had been a big fan, too. Especially on that one night Alissa had been conceived.

"Horrible about what happened to him. That bull nearly killed him."

Kelly nodded. It had happened just after Alissa was born. Trent had taken a bad throw, but then the bull gored him and tap-danced on his legs before they could get him free. His oh, so promising career was over. She'd reached out to him again after she heard, but his continued silence had made his point very clear.

He'd never once called to ask about his daughter.

Kelly might be able to handle seeing him again. However, wasn't she obligated to tell Trent that Alissa was the child he'd never wanted all those years ago? Alissa looked just like him. Not only did she inherit his stunning blue eyes, but Kelly also saw hints of Trent in the shape of her nose and chin. She would have to demand that he keep it a secret. He'd had his chance and he blew it. It had been one glorious fun-filled night of sex and passion and Kelly thought about it more often than was healthy. It had given her Alissa, though, so Kelly couldn't regret it.

Trent being in Last Stand was a complication her family didn't need. Her father's temper would explode if he found out that it had been his idol who'd knocked up his daughter. His health was fragile enough as it was. But more important, she was afraid Alissa would get hurt if she found out Trent hadn't wanted her.

"I was thinking about going down in August," Kelly said. "Alissa won't be starting kindergarten until next year, but if I want to get her into a good school down there, it would help if she attended some more preschool classes this summer. I could book her for a July session, and that way I can get things in order here so the move to Texas would be seamless." And it gave Trent plenty of time to get out of Last Stand and go back to wherever he called home nowadays.

"Nonsense. Go now. It's not like you're packing up a house. I'll ship you your things. Take a few big bags and get on a plane and go. Be with your sisters and help your parents. Don't let Alissa miss out on her first rodeo." Candace gave her a disapproving look. Kelly had deliberately not gone to a rodeo since she and Trent had hooked up. Too many memories, both good and bad, got dredged up.

She just wished Trent hadn't been such a douchebag when she found out she was pregnant. He made her feel like a gold-digging buckle bunny by not returning her calls or acknowledging his part in the consequences.

But not being at the ranch right now was gnawing away at her. She wanted to see her family again. She wanted to pitch in and help and maybe heal her damaged relationship with her parents for good. Was she going to let a one-night stand keep her from that?

Hell, no.

She probably wouldn't even see Trent up close and personal. There was no reason to point him out in the crowd to Alissa. She could handle seeing him in the arena from a safe distance in the rodeo stands. And after a nice day watching the events, she would go back to the ranch and continue on with her plans for a portrait studio. Her fingers itched to look at the ideas she had drawn up when she should have been working on one of Candace's wedding projects.

Kelly wondered if she'd have the temperament to run a business on her father's land where they would go head-to-head every day over every little thing. Maybe a better idea would be to stay until the business was up and running and then hire a photographer and manager she could trust. Once there was some new money coming in, Kelly wouldn't have to feel obligated to stay. She and Alissa could come back home. Home to New York. They'd made a new life here, free of bull riders and bullheaded men. With some business experience under her belt and some extra money for rent, there was no reason why Sullivan Portraits couldn't have a West Coast and an East Coast location. It didn't have to be in Manhattan.

"You're all right handling everything here without me?" Kelly asked, already knowing the answer.

"When are you leaving?" Candace said.

"Day after tomorrow."

Chapter Two

TRENT CAMPBELL LEANED against the rodeo stand and looked around, trying not to see himself in every corner of the arena—a younger version of himself. One that didn't walk with a limp or have constant pain in his side and hip. Closing his eyes, he could hear the crowd and the excitement in the air. A grudging smile pulled up his lips. Maybe he was also looking for a sultry strawberry blonde with eyes like hot chocolate and a sweet, kissable mouth.

Kelly.

Trent sighed. He never got her last name, but she had been in the stands six years ago. And later that night, she had been in his bed. Then life happened, and his phone got stolen with all his contacts. And just like that, she was gone.

She walks in beauty, like the night.

His physical therapist had made him listen and memorize poetry. Some lines stuck with him more than others. He had never seen Kelly again, but some days, she haunted him like the poetry did.

"You doing okay, kid?" his manager, Billy King asked, coming up behind him.

"Bittersweet memories," he replied. Kelly was B.A.—

before the accident. All the good things in his life happened B.A. He was wondering if there was life A.A.—after the accident. So far, he wasn't impressed.

"You should still be using your cane."

"I don't need it." Trent fought to keep his voice mild, but all he wanted to do was snarl.

"Have you been out to the ranch yet? The barn is up and the pen is finished. And they're putting the final touches on the studio. It looks great. Just like you requested."

"Not yet." The moment Trent walked onto the Three Sisters Ranch, his career as a professional bull rider was over, and his new career as a business owner would begin. Mentally, anyway. Physically, a Mexican fighting bull named Corazon del Diablo had taken care of that five years ago. "I want to get through the rodeo first."

"You're going to be able to hit the ground running. The schoolhouse is just about done. My crew is installing the carpets once the paint is dry on the walls. Make sure you talk up your school at the rodeo. You want to bring in the local boys and girls first. They'll be your bread and butter. Who wouldn't want to learn how to ride a bull from a professional bull rider?" Billy clapped him on the back. "Your name is still good around here."

Around here, yeah? Most people seemed to have forgotten him when he was riding a hospital bed instead of a bull. And the years of rehab while he learned to walk again had driven away everyone else. To be fair, he hadn't been the easiest person to be around. He practically became a hermit. It had been just him and Billy for five years straight. Still, he got the occasional fan letter and in local rodeos like this, he was a big draw. Even if he couldn't ride a bull.

"You need to order the equipment and the gear. Not to mention bucking stock. We've got a tight budget."

"I've got a plan, Billy. You don't have to micromanage me." This time, Trent couldn't keep the edge out of his voice. He knew Billy was only trying to help, and that Billy was worried about him sinking back into the deep depression that had hooked him recently.

While Trent was recovering, he had a goal and he had thrown himself into it wholeheartedly. The doctors said he couldn't walk? Bullshit. The doctors said he couldn't ride? Watch him. But once he had done that, taking his recovery as far as he could go, there had been nothing left. Who the hell was he, if he couldn't ride a bull? It was all he had ever wanted to do since he saw his first rodeo. He missed the adrenaline, the feeling that he was living on the edge, the roar of the crowd, the excitement. Everyday life was dull and colorless in comparison. There was no poetry in the mundane world.

Billy had offered to hire him as a talent scout, but Trent didn't want to leech off him. Billy was the closest thing he had to a father. His own father had left his mother when he was a baby. Trent didn't even know the man's name. And his mother had long since drunk herself to death, shortly before his sixteenth birthday. If it hadn't been for Billy, Trent's dream of becoming a rodeo cowboy would have lasted eight seconds, if that.

"Sorry," Trent grumbled out.

"It's okay, hoss." Billy gripped his shoulder and shook it good-naturedly. "I'm going to get the schedule of events and hammer down what they want you to do. You up to riding into the arena?"

"Of course."

Billy rolled his eyes. Of course, it hadn't been a consideration a year ago. The answer would have been: *No. Hell, no. Are you crazy?* But Trent had put himself through agony and countless hours of failure. He could get up into the saddle and stay there. Dismounting was still a challenge, though. Sometimes his leg wouldn't hold him, especially if the horse wasn't well trained. Riding wasn't fun and he didn't enjoy it anymore, and oh yeah, it hurt like a bitch. But he'd damned well ride into this arena, holding the Texas flag. He didn't care if he had to ice his hip and keep off his feet for two days afterward. There was some shit you just had to do.

"Should I put you on the roster as well?" Billy said, sardonically.

Trent smirked. "Don't tempt me." His eyes cut to the empty holding pens and the stalls. It would hurt. The fall would really set him back unless he landed just right, and even then, it was risky. He had no illusions he could stay on for eight seconds, unless the bull was having an off day. Still to feel that energy one more time, it might be worth it.

"I'll break your other leg," Billy muttered and walked away.

Looking around one last time, Trent nodded. He didn't have anything to prove. His body had limitations. It wasn't a crime to admit that.

Close the book on this chapter of your life, already.

"It's done." Pushing away from the stands, he forced himself to walk slowly away, concentrating on every step. This was his decision. Rodeo was in his blood, even if he couldn't compete anymore.

He was opening up a bull-riding school, leasing the land from a local ranch that was in trouble. Last Stand had given him so much, he was glad to give back a little. Billy had forced him to invest half of his purse every time he won. Good thing, too. It paid his medical bills that weren't covered by insurance and had allowed him to live modestly while he recovered.

But it wasn't a bottomless well. He needed to make some money and the idea of a school had broken through that black fog of depression like nothing else had. He had enough left to set up the school and start training youths. Trent hoped to obtain a few small business loans to keep him afloat while more students came in, so he could continue on with the lease. It was going to be a struggle, but if he could ride a horse after being stomped on by a two-thousand-pound bull, he could do anything.

At least, he hoped so.

Getting into his car, Trent adjusted the seat to better support his back. He popped two aspirin and washed them down with the last of the water in his water bottle. It was warm from being in the car, but the late June heat hadn't made it unbearable. He missed his truck. It had a cooler for beverages in the center console. But he'd had to sell it. Maybe he'd get another one now that he could get in it without a crane and four guys pushing.

He didn't want to go back to the hotel yet, so he turned onto Hickory and passed the statue of Asa Fuhrmann outside of the library and nodded respectfully at it. Asa was a hero of the Texas Revolution who'd died so the people of this town could hold off Santa Anna's troops. Trent noticed the statue had taken some damage and wondered what had happened.

Driving though Main Street was like driving back through time to his high school days. While there were a few new stores and buildings, the feel of the place was the same. He turned down Laurel and passed the high school. Parking in the lot, he could hear the sounds of the football team practicing.

He was considering getting out of the car and walking down to the field to take a look at this year's team, when he heard the whoop of a police siren. Glancing into his rearview mirror, he saw the squad car behind him. The officer got out of his car and sauntered up to his driver's side window.

"There a problem, Officer?" he drawled, hiding his smirk.

"You mean aside from the fact that you didn't use a telephone to let us know you're in town or stop by and say hello?" Pete Velasquez, one of his high school buddies, leaned his arm on the hood of the car and peered in at him.

"I hate talking on the phone, and I just got here."

"Have you eaten lunch yet?"

Trent's stomach growled. "Depends. Is your wife cooking?"

"Every day." Pete patted his stomach. "That's why I got

fat."

"You can just have one bowl of pozole, you know."

Pete shook his head. "I don't need that type of negativity in my life. That's crazy talk. You coming or what?"

"Best offer I had in a long while."

"Let's see you eat one bowl," Pete muttered and got back into his squad car.

Trent followed his friend home, even though he knew the way by heart. Pete lived on the corner of Honeysuckle and Hickory in his mother's duplex. Trent had spent many nights on their couch growing up, and still dreamed about Pete's mom's *frijoles de la olla*. Pete had tried his hand as bullfighter for a while, but gave up and became a cop instead. He joked it was safer chasing armed criminals than ornery bulls. He might not be wrong.

Pete looked him up and down as he got out of the car. Trent was careful not to wince in pain and forced himself to walk so it looked effortless. He set his jaw and walked up the three small stairs to the porch, only having to hold the railing once. He usually wasn't this bad, but the long car ride from Houston had almost done him in.

"You look better than last year." Pete held the front door for him. "We were worried about you. I tried to call you, but the phone kept ringing and eventually we figured your answering machine was full."

"I don't have an answering machine." Trent walked inside the house. "The nineties called—they want their technology back."

"Voice mail, whatever." Pete waved his hand in dismissal.

"Trent?"

He looked up just in time to receive a bone-crushing hug that had nothing on Corazon del Diablo. Only this time, he relished it and returned the hug with enthusiasm.

"Oh *mijo*, it's so good to see you."

"Hi, Mrs. V.," Trent said, appalled at how husky his voice sounded.

Only Pete's mother and Billy called him son. He wished he had known his father. He wished his mother was still alive. Or that she had been sober more than drunk while she was. Growing up, he'd wanted a large family like Pete's. And looking around the comfortable house, he realized he wanted what Pete had—a wife, kids, a loving family…a steady job. Trent gave a weak chuckle.

She thrust him away at arm's length and looked him over as well. "Thank the Lord, you're all right. You had us worried. No word for months. It was like you dropped off the planet. Come inside, eat."

"Hi, Trent." Pete's wife, Serena, leaned up against the kitchen doorway.

He brushed a kiss on her cheek before sitting down at the table. "Thank you for having me."

Pete snorted. "You think you're a guest? You're doing dishes afterward, because I have to get back to work."

Mrs. V. put a large basket of tortillas on the table. Trent could feel the warmth coming off them. When was the last time he had a home-cooked meal? Probably the last time he was here.

Serena served a platter of pulled chicken and steak and Mrs. V. followed up with a plate of shredded cheeses and grilled peppers and onions.

"Do you need any help?" he asked Mrs. V., as Pete was already digging in.

"No, start without us. I just need to grab the condiments."

She didn't have to tell him twice. He took a tortilla and piled on everything on the table. He even managed to roll it so he didn't spill it all down his shirt after the first bite.

Once the first fajita went down, Trent started making another one. Pete caught his eye and laughed. "Just one, huh?"

"Why have you stayed away so long, *mijo*?" Mrs. V. asked.

"It's been a tough road trying to learn to ride again. A lot of PT. I was off the grid for a long time, just concentrating on my recovery. After that—" Trent shrugged. "It became habit not to be attached to my phone or even one place for very long."

"How long are you staying? Just for the rodeo?" Serena asked.

Trent took a deep breath. "Actually, I'm opening up a bull-riding school in Last Stand."

Serena squealed and came around the table to hug him. "I'm so glad."

"That's great news," Pete said. "Where's it going to be?"

"I've leased some land over at the Three Sisters Ranch."

"Oh," Serena said, wincing. "Good luck with that. The

old man is challenging, to say the least. He'll be all up in your Kool-Aid."

Shrugging, Trent added a dollop of salsa to the fajita. "He can't be as ornery as a bull."

"He's close," Mrs. V. said. "He drove his poor daughters off, one by one."

"I didn't know he had daughters," Trent said.

"They were about four years younger than us," Pete said.

"One of them lives in New York," Mrs. V. said. "Another one is in Africa or someplace, and the last one works at a dressage ranch in Kentucky. I speak to Sarah, their mom, in the grocery store. The ranch has been struggling for a couple of years. I heard that they're allowing a game hunter to come in for the hogs and white tails. I think he's going to set up a lodge on the back forty."

"I can work around that," Trent said. "The school is up by the road so there's easier access. According to Billy, all I need are students."

"Are you going to have bucking stock?" Pete asked.

And that.

The thought made the hair on Trent's neck stand up. Picturing himself in the chute was one thing. Facing down a bull again was another. He forced himself to meet Pete's eyes and shrugged. "Yeah, eventually. Right now, I'm just taking beginners. I'm getting training units for practicing technique."

"Training unit?" Pete asked, his mouth full. His mother smacked him. "We used to use a fifty-gallon drum on a spring."

"These are a little more sophisticated than that."

"Well, la di da." Pete rolled his eyes.

"Are they like the mechanical bulls in the bars?" Serena said.

"No," Trent said, amused. "But maybe if things go well, I'll get one of those and take them around to fairs to drum up business. Anyway, I got a sweet deal on helmets and flak jackets with my name and logo on them. I haven't decided if I want to sell them separately or include them in the price of tuition."

"Why not both?" Mrs. V. asked.

Good idea.

They talked for a bit more, catching him up on the local gossip. But all too soon, Pete pushed back from the table. "Well, I got to go back to work. Feel free to stay as long as you want, Trent. I was serious about the dishes." He pointed in the kitchen.

"Oh stop," Serena said. "We have a dishwasher."

"Are you sure?" Trent asked.

She nodded.

"Well then, I should get going too."

Getting up from the table, he hugged Serena and then Mrs. V., watching with a little jealousy as Pete gave his wife a passionate kiss. There hadn't been a lot of time for romance while he was working his way through the rankings. He thought again of the mysterious Kelly. After his phone got stolen, there had been no way to reach her. Maybe, he'd see her this year at the rodeo.

They'd had one of the best nights of his life after the Last

Stand Rodeo about six year ago. He'd been back a few times since, but he never saw her in the stands. It had been a long shot, and he probably hadn't been ready for a relationship while he was still trying to walk normally and get back on a horse, anyway. Still, Trent would've loved to have seen her pretty smile again. He'd dreamed of her, and of that night, many times since.

"You need to come back and see Marisol and Alejandro," Mrs. V. said, showing him a picture of her grandkids who were in middle school.

"I will."

That was another thing he'd never had time for. Maybe, in this new chapter of his life, there would be.

Chapter Three

A S SHE DROVE the rental car through the gates of the Three Sisters Ranch, Kelly looked to her left, half-expecting and half-hoping to see one of her sisters galloping over to greet them. But instead, she saw a new building with a barn and pen attached to it. There were workmen milling around the site and if she hadn't had Alissa with her, she would have stopped to see what was going on.

That better not be the hunting lodge. It was too close to the ranch house and the road. The game animals were farther back anyway. It didn't make sense to build a hunting lodge this far up.

As she drove down the long driveway, though, that had been the only activity going on. It was like a ghost ranch. Everything else was quiet, except for the crunch of gravel under her tires and Alissa's iPad playing *Sesame Street*.

Today's show is sponsored by the letter W.

Why was she here again?

Why did she think she could do this? And where the hell were her sisters?

Kelly tried to come to terms with her brooding thoughts and the turmoil of emotions swirling through her. She hadn't expected to be so upset, but the feelings had started as soon as they'd landed. It wasn't like this when they came back for Thanksgiving or Christmas. Maybe because this time she was playing with the idea of making this permanent.

Her own business would be something to be proud of and help her get rid of the black cloud over her life. The shame surprised her. She didn't have anything to be ashamed about. So what, if she had gotten pregnant? So what, if it was with a rodeo star who left without a backward glance? So what, if her father had looked at her with disappointment up until he'd thrown her out?

"I want to see the horses," Alissa said. "Where are the cows?"

"You will," Kelly assured her. "The cows, though, are grazing in one of the back pastures. You probably won't see them until later tonight."

Alissa poked her bottom lip out. She had been a trooper for the flight and the drive, but Kelly's mommy senses were tingling. There was a tantrum on the horizon and her blonde-haired, blue-eyed angel was seconds away from turning into the demon child from hell.

"But you may get to see the kittens in the barn."

That nipped the tantrum in the bud. If only everything could be solved by kittens. Alissa's face cleared and she gave a big yawn, but went back to receiving instructions from the mother ship—or whatever Big Bird was saying. Kelly figured the kittens had bought her fifteen minutes of peace. But that was all she needed.

Parking outside of the garage, Kelly noticed all the little things she hadn't before. The flower beds surrounding the house were neglected. The lawn looked parched. There was a tractor by the barn that had seen better days, and an ATV with half its engine on a sheet next to it.

"You made good time from the airport." Her mother stepped out on the porch, wiping her hands on her apron. She was a tall and sturdy woman, with pretty features and graying hair. Every now and then, Kelly got a glimpse of her when she looked into the mirror.

"MeMaw!" Alissa flew up the stairs, launching herself at her grandmother.

"Easy," Kelly warned, but Sarah Sullivan was made of sterner stuff than that.

She swung her granddaughter around and then set her on her feet. "Come on inside. I've made chocolate chip cookies just for you."

And just like that, Kelly was alone by the car. "Nice to see you, too. The flight was long. And the drive was longer. I'm fine. How are you?" she said to the empty air.

After wrestling their bags out of the car, Kelly hauled them up onto the porch and then carried them inside where her father took them immediately out of her hands. "Dad, be careful. They're heavy."

He had aged. He looked so old. Frail almost. Growing up, she never remembered her father as ever being sick—well, more truthfully, he never admitted it. Looking him over with a critical eye, she saw he did look tired and pale.

"I got it," he said, pulling away when she went to take

the heaviest one back.

"Let me help."

"No," he snapped, showing the usual piss and vinegar she had grown up with. "I can damn well do it on my own."

She watched him struggle with the bags upstairs to the bedroom she had used as a child. She and Alissa would share it for the time being.

"Hello," she said to the empty foyer. "It's good to be back."

Was it? Was it really?

The emotional roller coaster she was on rivaled the Texas Giant at Six Flags, Arlington. Rubbing the back of her neck, she went into the large kitchen where her mother was fussing over Alissa. Kelly could see that Alissa had two cookies, a yogurt and a glass of milk.

"Hi, Mom," she said, kissing her on the cheek. "Are Janice and Emily here yet?"

"No, you're the first. Janice had a show this weekend, so she's coming Monday and I'm not sure when Emily is getting here. She was having a hard time getting a flight out." Sarah wiped her hands on her apron. "I hope everything is going to be all right."

"Of course, it will," her father said, bursting into the room and tickling a giggling Alissa. "Why wouldn't it? All my girls are going to be home. I can't wait to go to the rodeo together."

Kelly hid a groan.

"Rodeo?" Alissa asked.

"You didn't tell her about the world-famous Last Stand

Rodeo?" her father said, incredulously.

"World-famous is stretching it a bit, Dad."

But he had launched into the same old stories that she'd heard a million times before, but they were new to Alissa. Kelly tried to listen and enjoy them, but the simmering resentment she had felt since he'd tossed her out, pregnant, kept coming to the surface.

"I'm so glad you're home," he said, shooting her a grin.

Anger flared inside her and Kelly tamped it down. *No. It's your home. You could throw me out anytime you want to and Mom would let you.*

Ugh, she'd thought she was over this, thought she'd moved past it, like her therapist said. But like that ugly kernel of jealousy, Kelly still ached from the betrayal. Deep down, she was still that pregnant girl, scared of her father's rage and gutted by her lover's indifference.

She didn't want to be that person anymore!

It was tough to be jealous of her own daughter, but Kelly remembered when she had all of her father's attention, and none of it had been laced with disappointment. At least Alissa would have her support when her father's mercurial mood changed.

Kelly sprung up and walked to the picture window overlooking the many acres. The back lot looked better cared for than the front. That was probably Nate's doing. Their foreman worked night and day to keep the ranch together. Now that her father was slowing down, Nate was probably doing double the work instead of asking for help. She'd make it a point to check with him tomorrow morning to see how he was holding up. Not that he'd tell her if he was struggling, but she could see for herself. Or maybe, she'd leave Nate entirely to Janice.

It was both strange to be back in Texas and at the same time, it was as if she'd never left. Forcing herself to think about her portrait studio, she went over a couple of important things she would need. She'd have to convince her parents to put in an access road and a parking lot. It had to be far enough from the main house and the ranch house to not be in the way, but it had to be easily accessible for road traffic.

Kelly stared out at the scrub brush and the unforgiving dirt outside the window. She was confident she could make the business work. It was going to take her meager savings and a lot of fast talking at the Last Stand Bank for a startup loan, but she could do it. She had excellent credit. But better than that, she had gone to high school with the bank manager. As soon as her sisters got here, they could begin. But did she really want to live here, at her father's whim again? Certainly not when she had Alissa to consider. Kelly had to demand a contract. And that wasn't going to go over well.

"Can I talk with you?" Sarah asked, coming up to her.

Nodding, Kelly accepted the glass of sweet tea her mother offered her, and sank into the couch.

"It's going to be good to have a full house again. It'll be like Christmas with all of us under one roof."

"If we don't kill each other." Kelly smirked.

"How's Candace?" Sarah poured herself a glass of iced tea. "My sister is another one who should come back home more often."

"She's the same. She's happy. She's very successful."

"All I'm saying is that if she built up her little business here, she wouldn't have to live in New York City," her mother said.

Sarah made it sound like New York City was synonymous with the pit of despair.

"I like it there."

"It's not home."

Kelly flinched. "It is to Candace. And maybe even to me and Alissa."

"No, you're back where you belong. I appreciate you coming back home. It means the world to us."

Kelly stiffened at the repeated use of the word home, but made an effort to ignore it. "We're family. Like I said on the phone, if you don't want to sell the ranch, we'll do everything in our power to keep that from happening."

"I hope it's enough." Her mother looked down at her lap and then looked up. "It has to be, right?"

"How much is the hunter bringing in?"

"Donovan Link? He's a nice man. He paid for three months upfront to hunt and bring some tours in. But I think he'll be a long-term renter. That's good news."

Kelly wasn't sure they wanted armed strangers wandering around the property, but that wasn't her decision. She could only hope Donovan Link knew what he was doing. "Is he building a hunting lodge? Is that what's up front?"

Rolling her eyes, Sarah said, "No. That's your father's bright idea. He wants to wait until all you girls are together so he only has to tell about it you once. He's so excited—just like a kid at Christmas. I don't even know whose building it is."

Kelly was intrigued, but she knew she'd get nothing out of her father until he was ready to tell them. "How are you paying for the new construction up there?"

"We aren't. Your father's surprise is."

The plot thickens.

"What if you have to sell in the meantime?"

"The buildings will be a part of the sales agreement."

"Are Dad's secret project and Donovan Link's money going to be enough to get you through the short term?"

"It'll buy us a few more months."

"Don't worry, Mom. Janice and Emily and I are on the case."

"I'll still worry. It's what I do. But I also trust you girls." Her mother smiled and looked out the window wistfully.

"I have an idea that could help. I want to talk to you and Dad about it."

"Frank? Come in here for a sec. Kelly wants to talk to us." *Gee, no pressure Ma, I just walked through the door.*

Kelly took a deep breath instead and clasped her hands in front of her when they began to shake.

"I want to see the kittens," Alissa mewled, sounding a little like a petulant kitten herself.

"My thing can wait," Kelly said quickly, glad for the excuse.

"You can tell us on the way to the barn." Her mother got up and Kelly was forced to follow.

Once outside, PawPaw and MeMaw grabbed each of Alissa's hands and swung her between them. Kelly winced. "Dad, be careful. She's heavy."

"She's light as a feather," he said, swinging her higher.

Kelly closed her eyes and concentrated on keeping her temper. There was probably an unwritten grandparents' law about this somewhere that allowed them to override her, but she didn't have to like it.

Once Alissa was set up in the barn, Kelly had to run back into the house for her camera. The sight of her daughter with little orange puff balls crawling all over was too cute an opportunity to miss.

"You could have used your cell phone," her father said, showing her his. "Mine takes great pictures."

"Mine takes better." She smiled at him and positioned the kittens for the perfect shot. Unfortunately, the phrase *herding cats* was accurate.

"You wanted to talk to us?" her father said. Kelly could sense he was at the end of his patience, so she reluctantly let go of the need for the perfect shot.

"I had an idea for the ranch." She walked out of the barn and was glad to see them follow. She didn't need to have Alissa hear the argument, if there was one. Oh, who was she kidding? These were her parents. Of course, there was going to be an argument.

"Alissa and I were thinking of moving to Last Stand, permanently." Kelly figured she'd soften them up with the good news.

Her mother reached down and gripped her father's hand.

"We're so happy to hear that."

"I tell you I'm selling the ranch and you want to move here?" her father said, his voice rising.

Here we go.

"I want to rent some land—like your hunter is doing—to build a photography studio. I'm going to open up a business selling portraits and my photography prints."

Frank blew out an exasperated snort. "No one is going to pay for that."

Gritting her teeth at his casual dismissal, Kelly forged on. "Aunt Candace is working some old contacts and I have excellent references from local schools in New York."

Her mother dropped her father's hand and nudged him with her elbow. "I think that's a wonderful idea."

Kelly felt relief tickle the back of her throat. Even though her sisters and she had suggested some ideas on how to save the ranch, Sarah had shot most of them down. Kelly was surprised to have her mother's support in this.

"But you don't need to pay us rent," Sarah said.

Kelly wanted to bang her head on the barn door. "That's the whole point of Alissa and me moving back to Last Stand. We'll rent the land from you and that will go toward the upkeep of the ranch."

Her father set his jaw.

She knew he was dying to say something along the lines of "I don't need your help." But he did. His own phone message said so.

"This won't do anything but delay the inevitable," he said in a resigned voice.

"Don't underestimate your daughters," her mother said, again surprising Kelly. "Between the three of them and Donovan, it could be just the spark we need."

Frank considered it. "I've got plans too, you know. Did you see that building up front?"

"Yeah." Kelly leaned forward wondering if he was going to tell her.

"That's going to be our big break. I'm charging him a fortune."

"Him who?" Kelly said.

"Nope. You got to wait until your sisters get here. I only want to tell this story once."

"It better be good, Frank," her mother said.

"It is." He smiled devilishly and for a moment, Kelly felt sixteen again.

"I need to get a pavilion and a gazebo. I think the southwest part of the ranch would be best so we can get the sunsets in the bridal pictures."

Sarah nodded. "That sounds beautiful."

"We need photographs to advertise. I'll take Pippi out and scout some locations tomorrow."

"She'll be happy to see you."

"I missed her, but she wouldn't fit in our apartment. It barely fits the three of us." Her horse was a strawberry roan with a temperament as sweet as can be.

Her father was getting restless. It was time to seal the deal. "You can just make a copy of the contract you gave to Donovan Link and I'll sign it."

Frank guffawed. "I don't need a contract from my baby

girl."

"I do," she said softly.

He shook his head. "Not necessary."

"It is to me," Kelly argued.

"I'll charge you what I'm charging Link, but when you can't swing the rent, don't worry about it." Her father walked back to the barn.

Kelly clenched her fists, but forced a smile. "You don't have to worry."

"I ain't worried." Her father put his thumbs through his belt loops. "I've got my girl's back. That's all I ever wanted."

"Dad." Kelly started to go after him, but her mother laid a hand on her arm and shook her head.

It wasn't a complete victory, but Kelly was optimistic. He wouldn't throw her out if she pissed him off again, not when Alissa was part of the deal. But she didn't quite believe it. She couldn't wait for her sisters to get here. She needed to talk to them.

When they went back to the barn, Alissa was asleep in the hay with the kittens coiled up into balls all over her. This time, Kelly got the shots she needed.

Frank insisted on carrying Alissa up to their room. Kelly hovered, afraid that he would drop her because toward the last few stairs he was straining and breathing hard. But he managed to put her on the air mattress in Kelly's old room without waking Alissa. She was sleeping soundly, snuggled up with her teddy bear.

After her parents went downstairs, Kelly considered joining Alissa in a nap. But she tossed and turned. She couldn't get comfortable and her mind wouldn't shut off. So she unpacked instead, setting up her computer equipment before she put their clothes away.

Her room hadn't changed since the day she left it six years ago. Kelly had taken everything she could carry, so the room was sparse. But her country fair ribbons for photography and her Rodeo Queen hat and sash were still lurking about.

The room was stifling, even with the fan in the window. Or maybe it was because Kelly couldn't breathe right since she'd come back to Texas. She hadn't been expecting the anxiety to eat away at her. She should just go to bed, but was too restless to turn in. She didn't want to hang out with her parents who were watching the news and bickering over politics. Her sisters weren't texting her back, and Kelly thought her head would explode if she didn't distract herself.

She watched Alissa sleep, checking her breathing like she did every night. Kelly always had a moment of anxiety until she saw Alissa's chest rise or fall or even better yet, hear her give out a sweet baby snore. Tucking Alissa in, she gave her darling little girl a kiss on her cheek.

"I won't let him hurt you," she whispered. Whatever happened with the ranch and her portrait studio, Kelly would shield her daughter from her father's wrath, if it ever decided to rear its ugly head again.

Frank Sullivan hadn't always been a short-tempered pain in the patootie. At least, not to her. For the first sixteen years of her life, he had been her hero. He had taught her to ride and clapped the loudest when she was nominated Rodeo

Queen when she was eighteen. Whenever he introduced her to people, she was his "beautiful daughter, Kelly." Janice had been his "smart daughter," which should have pissed her off but didn't. As a teenager, it had seemed a better deal to be pretty rather than a brainiac. Emily was "the baby." Or as Frank introduced her, "My baby girl, Emily."

After Kelly got pregnant, she became just "his eldest daughter." Growing up, she'd had wrapped him around her little finger. All her sisters did. He'd been a softie where they were concerned. That was probably why she'd never thought he'd go through with his ultimatum. And why it still affected her, even after they had made amends.

She needed to get out of this house. She grabbed her keys and went downstairs.

"I'm going out," she called to her parents from the doorway.

"Where are you heading?" her mother said.

"Why? Do you need me to pick up something?"

"No, I was just wondering if we should stay up and wait for you."

"No." Kelly gave them a wave over her shoulder and hurried out the door. She wasn't sure why that made her feel like a rebellious teenager or why she just couldn't tell her parents she was going to the Last Stand Saloon for a drink.

She didn't want to deal with her father's disapproval any more today or get into an argument with her parents. She had feet of clay. She wasn't perfect. And she wanted a tequila shot like she wanted her next breath.

The saloon was just how she remembered it, dark and

noisy with a local crowd that she was surprised she fit back in with. Kelly found herself chatting with some old friends—Zoraya and Tabitha, from high school—and sharing a pitcher of Alabama slammers. Mixed with the tequila shooters, it was going to be a rough morning tomorrow, but Kelly didn't have enough left in her to care.

"Oh wow, would you look who just walked in," Zoraya said, fanning herself.

Tabitha looked up. "And he's coming this way."

Kelly threw back a shot of tequila. And when she looked up, Trent Campbell was making his way toward them. Her entire body clenched, then flushed, and she started to shake. She almost knocked the shot glass off the table when she put it down.

At first glance, he hadn't changed at all. If she hadn't known he'd been crushed by an angry bull, she wouldn't have looked twice. But now that she did, she could see the faint limp. He was a tall drink of water with longish brown hair that fell in sexy waves around his face. He still had rangy muscles and a killer smile.

Life was not fair that he was as sizzling hot six years later in a bar as he'd been winning the purse for longest bull ride at the Last Stand Rodeo. His electric-blue eyes burned with an intensity that sent a shiver through her. Little laugh lines warred with other, harsher lines around his sensual mouth. Yeah, he had aged a bit, but he was like a fine wine. A very fine wine. She didn't know what would be worse, if he recognized her—or if he didn't.

"Have we met?" he asked in that deep honeyed voice that

still had the power to make her toes curl in her boots.

Kelly wished she had brushed her hair, chewed a mint, something to stop a crushing wave of self-consciousness that made her mute. Did she look so different? Had having a child changed her so much? Had she been just one woman in a line of forgettable one-night stands? He'd changed her life, and she might not have even registered as important in his. Anger and resentment battled for control, along with the ridiculous urge to burst into tears. She was on the roller coaster again, this time shooting down so fast, she left her stomach at the peak.

Trent held out his hand and she shook it on instinct, but the rasp of his calloused palm covering hers made her catch her breath and look up at him. Familiar blue eyes smiled into hers.

"Kelly? Is that you?" he said.

Relief washed over her, leaving her feeling weak and dazed. He had remembered her.

"How do you two know each other?" Zoraya asked, putting out her own hand.

Panic flared through her at the thought that her friends might gush about her having a crush on him all through high school, but then Tabitha saved her by answering, "We were at every one of your rodeos, Trent. You probably remember us from the stands."

Yeah, let's go with that. Gratitude made her head spin more. She wasn't sure what she was feeling, but she thought another shot of tequila would help.

"That must be it," he said. "Can I have this dance?"

No one was dancing—just milling around, bopping to the jukebox. But her body engaged before her brain could and she shot to her feet. He led her out into the middle of the room that served as a dance floor on occasion. Then before she could process that she was going to be alone with the father of her child, he pulled her in close.

He smiled at her and she was transported back to her twenty-second birthday, when that same roguish grin had her good intentions dropping almost as fast as her panties.

She shook herself out of her daze. Trent Campbell was sexy as hell, but she knew from personal experience that he was a love 'em and leave 'em type.

"Remember me?" Trent whispered into her ear, as they swayed to the jukebox.

Kelly forced down a hysterical giggle. *Only every time I look into your daughter's eyes.* "Yeah, I seem to recall seeing you around here a few times." He smelled like expensive cologne and she wanted to burrow her face in his chest and lick every inch of him. She hoped that was the liquor talking, but she had a notion that she'd be feeling the same way even without the tequila.

"My name is Trent Campbell." He held her tight against him. It was getting hard to think straight. It felt so good to be in his arms, like she could let go of every problem and he'd take care of them for her.

"I know. I was just teasing," she said, catching her breath when he nuzzled her cheek. "I have very fond memories of being with you."

He rubbed against her and she felt how hard he was.

"Very fond," she whispered. Should she tell him? Would he ask? Kelly swallowed hard. If he asked, she would tell him about his daughter. If he didn't, he didn't deserve to know.

"I've been looking for you. Where have you been?" Trent brushed a kiss against her temple.

"You had my number," she said shakily.

"My phone was stolen."

Kelly tensed. "When?"

"A couple of months after I saw you."

Well, that explained why he hadn't picked up his phone when she'd called after she'd peed on the stick and found out she was pregnant. "But you got my messages, right?"

"Not a one."

She stumbled and gripped him in a panic.

"You all right, darlin'?"

No. She wasn't all right. Was he putting her on? "Your manager, what's his name?"

"Billy? Billy King?"

"Yeah," she said. "I called him looking for you."

He drew back in surprise and smiled at her. "You did?"

Nodding, she stared into his eyes. They were happy, not a shade of realization in them that she'd had his daughter.

"I'm sorry, but he never told me. To be fair, I was in a bad place. They thought I'd be in a wheelchair for the rest of my life."

"He didn't tell you anything?"

Trent shook his head. "I wasn't talking to a lot of people back then. Honestly, I was a bastard to everyone who tried to help me. Self-pity is a terrible thing. I eventually snapped out of it."

"Oh." Her legs were weak and she leaned more against him for support. Reality crashed down on her, trying to rewrite history. Had she capitulated and told her father that Alissa was Trent's, he would have ripped the country apart to find Trent and demand he man up and take care of his daughter, rodeo schedule or no. Billy King wouldn't have been able to stonewall Frank Sullivan. Hell, nothing would have stopped her father until he'd found Trent and confronted him with his responsibilities. Kelly wouldn't have been exiled. Trent would have known he had a daughter. And Alissa would know who her father was. It was even possible that Trent might not have ridden the bull that crippled him.

Her pride had caused this. She'd assumed Trent had ghosted her. Why hadn't she tried harder? Why hadn't she demanded he man up and support their daughter? Was it because her father hadn't supported her and she wanted to prove something?

"I never forgot about you," he said, trailing his fingertips over her cheek.

That made it worse.

"I never forgot about you either." What the hell was she going to do?

"Would you like to go somewhere a little more private and talk?"

Did she?

Not tonight. She had to tell him, and soon. It had to be soon. But not when she was half-drunk, guilt-ridden, jet-lagged, and so horny she could spit. "I just flew in from New York and it's starting to catch up to me. I should just go home." *To New York.*

He frowned. "Who's your designated driver?"

Closing her eyes, she thumped her forehead on his chest. "I kind of don't have one."

"I'll take you home. Where are you staying?"

Oh hell no. What if Alissa was up? What if her father was? "No, that's okay. I'll just hang out here."

"I don't mind. It'll give us some quiet time to talk."

"I'll probably fall asleep on you," she joked.

"Mmm," he purred in her ear. "I'd like that."

He revved her up more with his voice than most men had with their kisses. She needed to get out of here and away from him before she did something stupid, like try for a little brother for Alissa or beg his forgiveness while she dissolved into a teary wreck.

"I'll get my purse." Reluctantly, she pulled away from him and headed back to the table where her high school friends were. "Um, I've got to go."

"Yeah, girl. We see that." Zoraya smiled at her, while Tabitha gave her two thumbs-up.

"We'll catch up later," Tabitha said. "Because we'll want to know all the details."

Kelly had a feeling all the details were going to come out, and it was going to shock a lot of people...including the man who was grinning seductively at her.

With a nod to Slater Highwater, who was tending bar, Trent put his arm around her and guided her out of the saloon.

The night air slapped her face and she shivered, glad for the warmth of his body next to her. She was surprised when he led her to a sedan instead of a pickup truck. But when he opened her door, she noticed he was leaning heavily on it. "Are you all right?"

"You bet." He winked at her and walked around to the driver side, limping slightly.

"How's your leg?" she asked when he strapped himself in.

Shrugging, he said, "I won't be able to ride a bull for eight seconds again. But aside from that, things are generally back to normal."

She caught the bitter twist of his lips before his expression changed. "I saw YouTube footage of the accident. You must have been so scared."

"I was in too much pain to be scared, but when I watched the video, I was terrified. I'd have been better off if a truck ran over me. You know, I don't even remember losing consciousness."

She put her hand on his arm. "I'm glad you're all right."

Trent covered her hand with his. "It took a while, but I got there. I had a lot of time to think these past few years. I wish things had been different between us."

Kelly didn't want to hear that he regretted their one-night stand. "Trent…"

He talked over her. "I ran around with a lot of women. I not only sowed my wild oats, I sowed everyone else's oats on the circuit as well."

"I really don't want to hear this," she said dryly.

"What I mean to say is, I regret it. I should have called you more, found out more about you. Tried to get together, more. I was young and stupid. I thought we had all the time in the world."

Oh no. He couldn't do this to her. She'd start to cry and she wasn't sure that she'd be able to stop. "It's all right. It wasn't the right time for us."

"How about now?"

Kelly caught her breath. "I've got a lot of things going on right now."

"Yeah," he sighed. "Me too." Trent put the car into gear and pulled out onto Main Street.

"You staying at the Bluebonnet Inn too?"

"No, with my parents. Do you know where the Three Sisters Ranch is?"

He did a quick double take. "Sullivan's place? Your dad is Frank Sullivan?"

"Oh God, what did he do now?" Kelly winced. "I'm so sorry if he's bothered you. He's a really big fan."

"He is?" Trent straightened up in his seat. "So, you're Kelly Sullivan. His oldest?"

The beautiful one, her mind filled in sardonically. "Yeah, I suppose I should have given you my last name."

"It would have made finding you easier, too."

Kelly closed her eyes as her stomach lurched.

"But I should have asked. At the very least, I should have found out where you were from. If I'd known you lived in Last Stand, I could have tracked you down sooner. I grew up here."

"I know," she said. Somewhere in her parents' house, there was a scrapbook of him.

Her father loved the rodeo. He was a bulldogger in his youth and had always wanted to ride them instead of wrestle them. But he never could stay on. Frank liked to tell the story about how he'd been thrown off in the chute. It hadn't been his thing as much as he'd wanted it to be. So he followed the riders like some men followed baseball players or football teams.

And the best rider to come out of Last Stand was Trent Campbell. Kelly had cut out every article in the paper about him. Saved all the rodeo programs he was in. One of these days she was going to show it to Alissa. The way things were going, that was going to happen sooner rather than later. "I was a big fan, too."

Trent smiled sheepishly. "I don't remember you from school."

"I was a few years behind you." She realized she still had her hand on his arm and she reluctantly took it away. He felt real and solid and she wanted him to hold her and tell her everything was going to be all right. Even though she knew she was on borrowed time.

Would Frank kick her out again? Would he kick Trent out? Her father needed their rent money too much to do it, but his pride might not let him be reasonable.

"I wanted nothing more than to leave this town in my back mirror in those days. It's the height of irony that here is where I'll end up."

Her throat closed and it was difficult to breathe again. "You're staying? In Last Stand?"

"Yeah, your daddy leased me some land and I'm starting a bull-riding school."

"He what?" Kelly flinched away from him. "He never mentioned that." Neither had her mother. Was that her father's surprise? She closed her eyes. Of course, it was. It was just like her father to keep this a secret. But if he knew he had Trent as a tenant, what was this nonsense about selling the ranch? "I thought my father was putting the ranch on the market."

"Yeah. When my manager first talked with him, he said your dad had wanted me to buy the ranch outright, but I don't have enough money for five thousand acres, or enough collateral for a bank loan. Maybe, if I was still on the circuit?" Trent shrugged. "Anyway, leasing was the next best thing. I've got a three-year contract, with an option to buy the plot of land at the end of it. I figure if it doesn't work out, I can move on and start up again in another city." He looked over at her. "Is something wrong?"

In three years, Alissa would be eight years old. Would she get to know her father, just to have him leave? Maybe she should keep her secret. After all, they all got on just fine without Trent knowing he had a daughter. No. No. That wasn't right. She sighed.

"It's all too much," she whispered.

"What is?" he said, kindly.

Shit. She had to think of a cover and fast. "The ranch," she blurted out. "First, he was going to sell. He summoned us all home to say goodbye to the ranch. So, my sisters and I came up with a plan to basically do what he just did with you, and parcel up the land until the ranch was profitable again."

"What kind of plan?" he asked, as he pulled up to the ranch's gate.

She gave him the code and the rusty doors slowly opened.

"As you can see the Three Sisters Ranch has seen better days. But the land has so much potential. The southwestern portion is a perfect location for my portrait studio. I'm a photographer. The gorgeous sunsets would make a great background to a bridal party shoot. I also had a few more ideas on picture packages with the local schools and sports teams. Maybe I could string for the local paper. I'm going to take a ton of shots on the Fourth of July." Kelly started to warm up to the topic. It was better than thinking about how to tell him about Alissa.

"You can make a living selling pictures?"

"People are going to pay big money for my shots. My sister Janice, however, thinks the middle section of the ranch would be an excellent women's retreat—a dudette ranch— where women can learn to rely on themselves and each other."

"Really?" he said skeptically.

"Yes, really. And my baby sister, Emily, thinks that the wildlife on the ranch needs to be studied and preserved, and wants to build a research center for the appreciation of the ranch's natural beauty." Kelly managed not to roll her eyes, but scowled when Trent smirked. She could make fun of Emily, but no one else could.

"That sounds nice."

"Yeah, I'm not sure how she's going to react to Donovan Link, though."

"Link is the hunter?"

"You know about that?"

Trent nodded. "Your father was upfront about that when I signed the paperwork six months ago. I've only seen pictures of the buildings. It looks nice. My manager said it's all ready for my bull-riding school. There's supposedly a barn, a studio and a corral."

"You mean that?" Kelly pointed.

"Yeah, I guess that's it." Trent parked. "I'd offer you a tour, but I don't have the keys."

"Six months?" she said numbly. "You signed six months ago?"

"Thereabouts. Why?"

"My father lied to get us down here, to get us sparked up to save the ranch." Kelly shook her head. "I feel like such an idiot. I can't believe I fell for it."

"Maybe at the time he told you, it was true."

"He left all of us voice mail messages a week ago that he was selling the ranch."

Trent put the car back in gear. "First I've heard of it. He still could be selling. As long as my lease is grandfathered in, that wouldn't change things. I'd just be paying rent to someone else."

"No, with the three of us paying rent, that buys him

some time. Hell, with your name and talent, you could probably save the ranch single-handedly with the people you bring in."

"Whoa, now. I'm not a superhero. I'm just an average guy."

"Not around here, you're not. And certainly not to my father. With you and Donovan, he didn't need my sisters and me to come home. He wasn't going to sell. Not right away."

"I'm sensing that doesn't make you happy."

Kelly put her hand on the door handle. "I don't like being misled."

"Yeah, I wouldn't like it either."

Guilt ate at her. Would he think she had misled him? God, her head hurt. She was really regretting the tequila. She paused before she got out of the car. "Sometimes, though, it's all a misunderstanding, a lack of communication, you know. Sure, you can point a finger of blame but what does that solve?" Kelly laughed nervously and wrung her hands. She wasn't talking about her father anymore. She was talking about herself. She didn't want Trent to blame her for not telling him about Alissa. She'd tried, damn it. And damn that stupid manager of his for keeping it from Trent.

Didn't anyone tell the truth anymore? At least Billy King had been a stranger. Her own father was playing games with his daughters' lives. If she let herself dwell on how he'd misled her and her sisters, how his call for help made them drop everything and run to him, she would explode. The ranch might still be in decline, but it wasn't in any immediate danger. Her parents were not selling. Not this year anyway. What were they up to? Did they even care that Emily wasn't done with her missionary work or that Janice was so well respected in her field, the dressage competitions asked for her by name?

Squinting at her, Trent said, "Sounds like you've forgiven your father in the space of two seconds. I'm worried you're going to get whiplash."

Kelly rubbed her temples. "I know. Like I said, I'm tired, jet-lagged and now a bit hungover. This has been quite the night."

"Sorry you didn't get to enjoy the buzz a bit more." He took her hand and kissed her palm.

Little tingles of joy shot through her.

"I'd like to see you again. Can I take you out for dinner tomorrow?"

She nodded. "Sure." It was going to be impossible to ignore him, with his school being on the same ranch her studio was going to be on. She'd figure out a way to set things right. Just not tonight. Kelly was ready to drop from exhaustion and emotion.

"Great." He leaned in and brushed his lips against hers. The kiss was soft and persuasive. She didn't want it to end. Leaning in, she cupped his face as their tongues tangled. She shifted closer when his hand slid up her shirt. Trent rubbed a slow circle over her back. Kelly arched like a kitten being stroked. He was wearing too many buttons on his shirt and her fingers were trembling too hard to undo them. Catching her hand in his, he held it while they kissed.

When he pulled away, she remained there with her eyes closed, still feeling the imprint of his mouth on hers.

"You better get inside," he growled. "Before I turn the car around and take you back to the Bluebonnet Inn."

It was tempting. So tempting. Six years ago, she would have done that in a heartbeat. Six years ago, she did. Opening her eyes as that realization hit her, she was trapped by the heated look in his eyes.

"I'll see you tomorrow," he said, and it sounded like a promise.

Kelly had to force herself to get out of the car before she did something everyone would regret in the morning—especially her daughter.

Chapter Four

TRENT REALIZED HE never got Kelly's number last night. Had he learned nothing? He'd been so shocked to see her in the bar, sitting there with her strawberry-blonde hair up in the same sassy ponytail he remembered from his erotic dreams. Holding her against him had made his brain short-circuit so his dick took over and tried to get her to go back to his hotel room. Then she hit him with the fact that she was a Sullivan, and then those kisses messed with his head. He felt like he was back on the circuit again, being bucked and shook all over the place. But for the first time in a long while, he woke up feeling like his old self.

At least this time, he knew where she lived. Billy was waiting for him in the breakfast nook of the hotel. He was already working on his laptop. Trent grabbed a kolache and an orange juice before joining him at the table.

"Hey, Billy, do you have the number for the Sullivan ranch or just Frank Sullivan's cell phone?"

"The ranch. He never gave me his cell phone."

"Give me the number. I'm going to call him." The waitress came around and poured him a cup of coffee. She was a pretty brunette and her name tag said, Maisie. "Thank you, darlin'."

"Sure thing, Trent. Can't wait to see you at the rodeo next Saturday."

"I'm just going to be announcing." Trent winced when Billy kicked him under the table.

"Looking forward to it." She winked and walked away with a sway in her step.

"You don't need any distractions like that," Billy said.

"That's the best kind of distraction," Trent said. "But you're right. I've got other priorities." One of them was Kelly Sullivan.

"Good. There's always going to be women wanting a piece of you."

"That's a heck of an attitude." Trent drank his coffee, feeling the last bit of sleep fall away as the caffeine hit his system.

Billy grunted. "If you knew how many women I've had calling me up with every excuse in the book trying to get close to you, you'd be cynical too."

"Yeah, I heard," Trent said, thinking about what Kelly said last night. It was irritating, but he knew Billy had only his best interests at heart. "Next time, let me decide who I want to talk to or not?"

"Whatever, stud. You need to concentrate on getting your life back before you go chasing the fillies. Or in this case, letting yourself getting roped like a calf."

"I can handle it. Now, do you have Sullivan's number or not?"

"I thought you were going to wait until after the rodeo."

Billy looked up from his laptop.

"Yeah, I decided to see what my money has been building these past few months. I figured I'd give the man a call
and introduce myself." Trent popped the kolache in his
mouth. Ooh, that had a little kick. Jalapeno sausage and
cheese. He'd been hoping for a fruit-filled one. Oh well,
sometimes you get the sweet, and sometimes you get the
heat.

Billy grunted and wrote the number on a napkin and slid
it over to him. Trent programmed it into his phone and
tucked the napkin into his pocket just in case. "I'll be right
back. If the waitress comes around again, have her fill up my
cup." He washed down the kolache with the rest of his
coffee.

Billy didn't acknowledge him, but Trent knew he'd
heard. They were used to each other, used to living in hotels,
motels and one memorable summer, on a tour bus together.
After Trent's mother died, the nights he didn't spend on the
Velasquez's sofa, he was with Billy. Some days that meant
hanging out with Billy's other rodeo clients. Some days that
meant eating stale vending machine crackers on a lumpy
hotel bed and sneaking Cinemax after dark when Billy wasn't
in the room.

They traveled across the country and the PBR took them
all over the world. He had ridden bulls throughout North
and South America. Most of the towns all meshed together,
but the days had been hard and the nights had been wild,
full of alcohol and easy sex. Trent was surprised how little he
missed those days. But the bull riding? He'd sell his soul for

another chance to ride. He dreamed of what he should have done differently that night on Corazon del Diablo. Even though he knew that every ride was different and you couldn't plan how the bull was going to jump, Trent wanted to try. His body had other plans, however. This morning, he'd been thrilled to lift himself out of the pool without making old man noises.

He couldn't remember a time when Billy wasn't micromanaging him. First it was making him get good grades in school so he wasn't cut from doing rodeo. Then it was as his manager. Lately, it had been as his nursemaid. It would have chafed, had it been anyone else. But Billy didn't have any qualms about doing whatever it took to make sure Trent had whatever he needed to survive and prosper.

Trent remembered one time Billy had even taken a punch for him. Trent had really deserved the punch too, but he'd been scheduled to ride Fury's Kiss that night. No one had gone eight seconds on that son of a bitch, but the odds were in his favor and he'd been flying high. Trent had been taking pictures with a stacked redhead and one thing led to another. He had no excuse except he was a young eighteen-year-old and she was pretty demanding. She never told him she was married, however. Or that her husband was a bullfighter in the ring that night. Billy had pushed him out of harm's way and had taken the shot on his shoulder instead of Trent taking it on the chin.

It was a good thing Trent had taken Fury's Kiss to the end and jumped off without a scratch, because he wasn't sure how enthusiastic the husband would have been about protecting Trent if he'd been thrown. Damn that seemed like another life. It could have been another person, for all that remained of that eighteen-year-old boy in Trent now. What would that kid have done if he knew that thirteen years later, he'd be wobbling like an old man and worried about bucking stock?

He would have laughed in disbelief and sneered.

What would that kid have done if he'd met Kelly sooner? Probably the same damned thing.

That kid had been an asshole. It helped that even though he couldn't ride a bull anymore, he had grown up a bit. The last thing he wanted was a string of one-night stands. He knew what he wanted and now that he'd found her, he wasn't going to let Kelly Sullivan out of his sight.

Going outside, he dialed Kelly's parents' number, feeling like a teenager.

"Hello?" an older woman's voice said.

"Hi, may I please speak to Kelly, ma'am?" Definitely high school.

"Who is this?"

Trent paused. He hadn't expected to be asked that. "My name is Trent Campbell, ma'am."

"The bull rider? Why do you want to speak with my daughter?"

"Mom, give me the phone."

He heard Kelly's voice and a minor scuffle. "I'm so sorry about that."

"Good morning, beautiful." He smiled, picturing her a little sleepy and grumpy.

"Good morning."

"Are you blushing?"

"No," she said hotly. "Well, maybe a little."

"Did I wake you?" He checked his watch. It was a little past nine, but she'd been jet-lagged. He probably should have waited another hour or so.

"No, I was up having breakfast. Mom made us blueberry pancakes. My favorite."

"Mine too." He wondered if her fingers were all sticky and if she tasted like maple syrup. He had to adjust himself when his cock swelled at the thought of licking her fingers clean. "How's your head?"

"Reminding me that I'm too old for tequila shots."

"You're never too old."

"Tell that to my headache." There was a bit of a pause and he heard her walk away from the din of the kitchen noises. "Thanks for driving me home last night."

"Anytime. Hey, about that, how about I swing by there later, and take you to pick up your car?"

"I'd like that. That's very kind of you."

"We can go to lunch afterward."

"Sure."

She sounded distracted.

"Is there something wrong?"

"No, no that's okay. I was going to go riding today before it got too hot, but I suppose that can wait until tomorrow."

"Why don't I come over now and we can ride together?" Trent knew he was being pushy, but there was something about her that made him want more.

"Sure," she said again, in that forced voice.

"Unless you have other plans."

"No, no, that's fine. Give me a few minutes. I have to take a shower and get dressed."

"Great."

Trent went back inside and took a second look at the kolaches. They weren't marked, so he grabbed another one from a different pile.

Sitting back down, he was happy to see the waitress had refilled his coffee. He bit into the Czech pastry tentatively. Bingo! Apricot.

"Any plans today?" Billy asked.

"I'm going to stop by the Three Sisters Ranch and take a look at the school. Got my keys?"

Fishing in his pocket, Billy tossed him a PBR key ring with two keys hanging off it. "Do you need me to come with you?"

"Nope," he said.

Billy handed him the schedule of events for the rodeo next week. "Here's what they want you to do."

"Pictures and autographs?" Trent said. "Me?"

"I'm sure you'll have a line around the arena."

"Hey, I'm going to be a judge for the mutton bustin'." Trent grinned.

"And you're going to be at the ceremony crowning the court."

"Piece of cake," Trent said, downing his cup of coffee.

"So you're meeting with Frank Sullivan?"

"Nope."

"No one was home?"

"I didn't speak with Frank. See ya later," he said to Billy, and dashed out of the hotel before Billy could ask him any more questions. He didn't want to get the "stay focused" lecture from Billy again this morning. Billy had always been hands-on in Trent's love life and it was starting to chafe. Billy once fired a nurse because he thought she was flirting with him too much. She had been, and Trent hadn't minded, but Billy didn't think that was too professional, so out she went.

On the drive over, Trent came to the awful conclusion that if they were going to go riding, he was going to have to mount and dismount in front of Kelly. Trent hoped his leg was up for it. He didn't want to make a bad impression on her by falling flat on his ass—or worse. The gate opened as his car approached it, which was a good thing because he had forgotten the code.

Driving past his new school, he was tempted to check it out. But he was more eager to see Kelly. When he got to the house, he was surprised to see her out front waiting for him. He had barely gotten out of the car, when she grabbed a hold of his arm and tugged him to the barn. "We should get going before my father realizes you're here. He'll talk your ear off and we'll never get rid of him."

"I do have to speak to him at some point, but you're right. This is our day."

She looked back over her shoulder and smiled tightly at him.

"Are you all right?" he asked. She was acting a little strange. "You're not regretting last night, are you?"

"What? Why? What happened last night? Oh, you mean the kiss." Her face softened. "No, I'm not regretting that. I just have a lot on my mind. I'm still processing what you told me last night about my father brokering a deal with you a half a year ago."

She guided two horses out of their stalls. One was a beautiful red roan and the other a palomino. She handed him the palomino's reins. "I don't know about this," he said.

"Should we take the ATV?"

His hip screamed, YES. His pride said, hell no. "No, it's just I'm not used to riding a horse that's prettier than me."

"She knows it too. Pippi is less vain." She patted her horse's neck affectionately. "I gave you my sister Emily's horse, Sunflower."

"You're kidding, right? She should be called Siren."

"Or Helen?" Kelly joked.

"Of Troy? The face that launched a thousand ships and burned the topless towers of Ilium?"

"You're pretty well read for a bull rider."

"I had to do something during recovery."

She launched herself into the saddle with the natural grace of someone who had been doing it all her life. He used to mount like that. Effortless.

It was now or never. He eyed Sunflower and the pretty thing eyed him back with a sweet, but dim look. That was something at least.

"Do you want a stepladder?" Kelly asked, concerned.

His hip went, YES, I DO. His pride went, hell no.

"Nah, I got this." *Please look away.* Of course, she didn't.

Trent gritted his teeth and put his foot in the stirrup, and swung his leg over. It wasn't the prettiest mount he'd ever done, but he was up there and he was planning on staying that way. He'd worry about dismounting when the time came.

As they rode out, he knew his jaw was going to hurt as much as his hip would. Trent was already planning on stopping by for a couple of twenty-pound bags of ice. Having a party? Yeah, a pity party. He was going to shiver in the tub with the ice around his leg and hip tonight. It was going to be worth it, though, just to see the sun shine through her hair.

"So, you read poetry while you were in physical therapy?" she asked, smiling at him.

"Listened to it on audio books, actually. The cadence of it helped me manage the pain. And if I was trying to memorize it at the same time, it took my mind off my body not working the way it should."

"I'd like for you to recite me poetry."

"Shall I peel you a grape and fan you with a palm frond too?" He grinned.

"Absolutely."

"I'm not sure you'd appreciate it," he teased.

"Trust me. I'd appreciate it. I'd probably fall asleep, though."

"I already told you, having you in my bed is quite all right with me."

"Even if I was sleeping?"

"You'd wake up eventually, and when you did…" He moved the horse closer to her so he could playfully tug on her ponytail. "Then, you'd be all mine."

She swatted his hand away and gave him a mock glare with her pretty chocolate-colored eyes. "You're a flirt."

"I'm trying anyway."

Kelly took them back around to the front of the ranch. "I didn't get a chance to tell my parents this morning that I knew about your school, but I figured you'd like to see it first before I show you around the rest of the ranch."

"Yeah, I'm pretty eager to go inside. I've had a crew working on it for months based on plans I modified. Like I've said, I've seen pictures, but it's something else to see it live."

"Let's look around." They headed closer to the building and paddock, riding in companionable silence for a few minutes. He was sore and unused to being on a horse, but he couldn't ask for a more gentle ride. He was starting to get the feel of it again, starting to feel normal.

"You'll probably want to get a turnoff from the main driveway and a parking lot." She pointed.

"Yeah, I can't have them park on either side of your driveway." Movement caught the corner of his eye and he looked back toward the barn. An ATV was coming their way.

"Oh shit," Kelly groaned.

"What?"

"That's my dad. Um, can you pretend that we just met

last night? He doesn't know that we have a past."

Trent smiled. "Sure thing."

"And I apologize for anything he says."

They reined in and waited for Frank to catch up with him. Trent noticed that the older man was a bit out of breath, but his eyes were shining when he hopped out of the ATV. "I know you," Frank said, coming in close and thrusting his hand out to Trent.

Trent shook it. "It's nice to meet you, Mr. Sullivan."

"How do you know my daughter?" Frank's smile looked like it could turn in a moment.

"Dad," Kelly warned.

"I was at the Last Stand Saloon last night, and your daughter and I got to talking."

"Trent was nice enough to drive me home after I'd had a few too many with my high school friends."

"I appreciate you taking care of my daughter," Frank said, nodding.

"He told me that you leased him this property for his rodeo school," Kelly said with enough tart sweetness in her voice that Trent winced.

"Yup."

"I thought you were going to sell. Isn't that what you said in your message?"

Frank shrugged. "We're not out of the woods yet. I wanted to make sure you and your sisters had a chance to say goodbye."

Kelly seemed somewhat mollified by that admission. "The girls and I have plans. We're not going to go down without a fight."

"Yeah," he snorted. "You want to spend money we don't have. Trent and Donovan at least are building on their own dime."

"So will we," Kelly said sharply.

"I'm going to need to put in an access road and parking lot. Does that suit you?" Trent said, jumping into the conversation.

Frank frowned, but then nodded. "I guess you got to do that. Where's your manager?"

"He's still eating breakfast," Trent said. "Kelly and I were just about to take a look at the place. Care to join us?"

"Sure thing. I've been keeping an eye out just to make sure things have been going as planned."

"Of course, you have," Kelly said dryly. They steered the horses over to the pen. She dismounted and flipped the reins in a loose knot over the paddock's pole.

He winked at Kelly. "He's not so bad," he said, as her father walked inside the barn without waiting for them.

She rolled her eyes. "Try living with him."

Trent waited until she turned to follow her father before he dismounted. When she went into the barn, Trent swung his leg over and stepped down from the saddle, leaning heavily on Sunflower. Thankfully, the horse didn't move and let him rest his weight against her while he got his balance. He let out a slow breath of relief. He hadn't fallen on his ass.

Pain shot up his bad leg and he had to lean on Sunflower until the stars in front of his eyes went away, but he could still walk.

"This here's nice, Trent." Frank came out of the barn and waited next to him as he figured out which key opened the studio door.

He finally got it open and they stepped inside. Frank found the light switch and flicked it on. It was just how he pictured it. The new carpet smell mixed in with paint fumes. He left the door open to air it out while they walked around.

"That's my office over there," Trent said to Kelly, pointing to a room with a cutout window. He needed to move his things here from storage.

"I see there's a couple of trophy cases," Frank said. "I can't wait to see them and all your ribbons."

He didn't want it to seem like he was bragging, so he said to Kelly, "I put those in here because I thought it would bring the teenagers in with their parents."

"Definitely," she said. "I'm a little astounded at how fast all of this went up. I hope my studio goes up this easy."

Frank snorted. "It's a lot of work, baby girl."

"I'm not going to saw boards and pound nails myself." Kelly looked up at him. "Not that I don't know how to do that, but I'm going to hire a construction crew."

"Not with my money, you're not."

"What money?" Kelly asked.

And just like that, Frank's face turned down and the menace in his eyes stiffened Trent's spine. "You watch your tone with me."

Kelly didn't seem the least bit fazed. "When they're done here, Trent, do you mind if I get some quotes?"

It took him a minute to catch up with what was going

on. Right. The construction crew. "I used Sykes. They're local." Trent walked them outside so they could get a closer look at the chutes and the gates that led out to the paddock.

"Bunch of punks," Frank muttered. "But I can't complain on the job they did. When's the bucking stock coming?"

That again. Trent was worried that the students would only come if they could see him bull ride. "I've got a couple of mini bulls coming in a few weeks for the kids. But we're going to use the trainers first on the teens and adults. It's important to me that we go over equipment, chute procedures, how to ride and dismount. That's all going to be done before they get on the bull, no matter how old or experienced they are." He gestured back to the studio. "I'm going to mount some televisions inside, as well, so they can review techniques and practice them on the riding machines."

Frank made a scoffing sound. "Is that how you did it?"

He'd just about had enough of Frank, but Trent didn't want to alienate Kelly's father. "No, sir, I made a pain in the ass of myself at the rodeos and PBR events. I worked as a bullfighter, rope puller, spotter, flank man, latch man, gate man…"

"I get it," Frank said. "You didn't learn it in a classroom is all I'm saying. You learned by doing."

"Dad, he's running a school so people can learn by doing in a safe and structured environment." Kelly put a light hand on Trent's back and he appreciated her support.

"You need a big bull. A real bastard." Frank clapped his hands and rubbed them together.

"Don't let my liability insurance company hear you say that."

Frank guffawed. "Just don't take it easy on these guys."

"I'll have different age groups and the lessons will be age appropriate."

"If you bore them, they ain't coming back."

"If they get hurt, they won't be back either."

Trent hadn't expected the awkward silence, but he wasn't unhappy about it.

"I'm looking forward to seeing what you can do here, son." Frank held out his hand and Trent shook it.

"Before you go, Dad, let's head down to the southwest. I want to show you what I think the best place is to put a gazebo for wedding and engagement pictures," Kelly said.

"I'll see it later," Frank said, waving his hand dismissively.

Kelly set her jaw.

"Trent, it was nice to finally meet you in person." He shook his hand again. "My daughters and I went to every rodeo you were in. We were big fans."

"You did?" Trent smiled at Kelly, who was blushing.

"So, we're honored to have your school here. If you need anything, just let me know. I'm going to head back in. The sun gets to me, lately."

"You want us to ride back in with you, Dad?" Kelly asked.

"Hell, no. I'm not some invalid who needs his hand held."

Trent tried to keep himself from tensing up. "Not that

there's anything wrong with that. Not too long ago, I was that invalid and I could have used all the hand-holding I could get."

"Dad," Kelly growled at him.

"'Scuse me, Trent. I didn't mean you. I meant an old man invalid. Anyhoo, I can see I stuck my foot in it, so I'll go. Stop by after your ride, if you want. Sarah puts on a nice lunch."

"We're going out for lunch," Kelly said.

"That right?" Frank brightened up.

"We have to get my car," Kelly said quickly.

"Oh." His face fell back into his normal expression. "Well then, I'll see you when I see you." He gave a half wave and went back outside.

"I am so sorry about that." Kelly slumped. "He's got all the tact and social grace of a bull."

"That's okay. I knew what he meant." But it did bother him that men like Frank would think less of him because of his injuries. It shouldn't, and maybe in a few hours it wouldn't, but right now, it chapped his ass. Mostly because it fueled his own thoughts about not fitting into a world when he wasn't a PBR star.

"Are you going to hire people to help you out?" she asked, wandering around the first floor.

"Eventually, but for right now, it's just me and Billy."

She scowled and looked away.

He wondered what he'd said to make her angry. "I need to get situated first. I've got equipment arriving that needs to be set up, but no revenue coming in. Once that happens, I probably will need to hire someone."

"That sounds great." She crossed her arms over her chest and looked around. "I think you're going to be very popular."

"Even if I don't have riding stock?"

There must have been something in his voice, because she dropped her arms and came in close to him. "Yeah, even if. You have a lot of fans and plenty of people are going to want to learn from the best."

"Well, they're going to have to settle for me."

"You are the best."

"I was," he said. "I'm not sure what I am anymore. I just hope I'm good enough."

"Of course, you are." Kelly looked up at him and he was momentarily distracted.

He wanted to kiss her again. Kiss her until they were both senseless and needing each other more than they needed their next breath. "I hope you're right. Otherwise, I'm going to have to consider another profession. And I think an office job would kill me faster than another bull ride."

"Don't say that." Kelly laid a hand on his arm.

Damn, but he liked it when she touched him.

He slid an arm around her waist and tugged her in closer. "We didn't get to dance for very long." She felt sweet in his arms.

"There's no music." Kelly lifted her head up, her lips parting.

He cupped her cheek and rubbed his thumb over her bottom lip. "Close your eyes. I bet you'll hear it."

Her eyes fluttered closed and a small smile played around her lips.

He couldn't resist her any longer. Kissing Kelly was even better in the daylight. Her mouth was sweet and eager on his. Tightening his grip, he backed her slowly against the nearest wall. She made a little sound of excitement and it went straight to his cock.

He had a flashback of making out with her, hard and fast in his truck after the rodeo six years ago. Trent had fingered her to a quick orgasm, while she nearly made him lose his mind with the best damn blow job he'd ever had. They barely made it to the hotel out of town before getting each other off again. Then they spent the whole night going slow to make up for the fast and furious fucking. Trent wanted that now. He'd take it slow or fast, whatever she wanted.

Rubbing against her, he wished she was wearing a skirt instead of sexy jeans that showed off her fantastic ass. Kelly parted her legs and he reached down and picked her up so she could wrap them around his waist.

His hip protested, but he ignored it. It was so worth the pain he was going to feel later. Kelly clutched at his shoulders and writhed against him. His mind whirled where to take them. The floor? Upstairs in the loft? Shit, he knew he should have had a couch delivered.

He carried her toward his office when he heard the horses snort and whinny and then the thundering of hooves. Letting Kelly slide down his body, he walked with her over to the door and peeked out. The horses had pulled the knots that had held the reins on the paddock fence free and were running back to the barn.

"Shit," he said. At least, they weren't heading toward the street.

Kelly laughed and then covered her mouth with a hand. "We're never going to catch them."

"It's a long walk back to the barn." He wasn't sure what he was going to do. His leg might not make it. He could call Billy, but he didn't want to talk business. They could call her father to come back and pick them up in the ATV, but he didn't want the man's pity. Not to mention he didn't want to explain what he'd been doing with his daughter while the horses made their escape.

"Guess we'd better get started," she said.

Man up, he told himself as they headed back.

She reached for his hand and squeezed it. "I'm sorry we got interrupted."

That made him smile. "Me too." He would love to invite her back to his hotel room after lunch, but there was no way he wanted her to see him curled up in pain. "I should get a futon and keep it upstairs."

"For morning trysts?" She eyed him. "You planning on making this a regular occurrence?"

"I'd like to. With you."

Kelly slung her arm around him. "Me too." But then she got quiet and moved away from him.

Trent wanted to get her playful side back, so he nudged her. "I'd rather fool around and nap than walk back to the ranch."

"And when my father came to look for us?" She batted

her eyelashes at him. "What then?"

"Do you think he'd buy that I was giving you bull-riding lessons?"

"Some kind of riding lessons, he'd believe."

"Kelly, you don't need lessons in that kind of riding. In fact, I'd like you to show me a few things." He was glad she'd shaken off whatever had dampened her spirits.

As they walked along, he realized that he wasn't feeling the pain in his hip as badly as he thought he would.

"I'm going to need to extend the road back this way and hope Nate doesn't get his feathers ruffled that we're disturbing his cattle," she said. "Otherwise, my customers will have to deal with the odor of cow flops."

"Who's Nate?" She spoke of him with admiration and he was wondering if Nate was someone he should be concerned about.

"He's the foreman. He's been with us forever, it seems. He came to the ranch when he was ten and worked his way up. He's like a brother to me in some respects."

That was good.

"Got a nice spread of land here," Trent said. "I can't quite picture what you're going to do, but I think you'll get a lot of people interested."

"The gazebo will be for pictures. You've seen how photogenic Pippi and Sunflower are. I might even get some ponies and advertise children photo packages. I bet there's even a market for head shots for local actors."

He chuckled. "Are you practicing that speech on me before you present it to your father?"

"Like he cares," she said with a sad smile. "I'm not doing it for him. I thought I was, but I think I want this business to succeed for me more. That said, I am definitely looking forward to helping the ranch get back on its feet again."

It wasn't so bad, strolling along with her like this. He liked listening to her voice. It was almost like poetry and it took his mind off how uncomfortable he was. As they walked on, though, Kelly got more and more distracted and her conversation trailed off. He'd been enjoying the walk, but as the barn came into sight and they saw their two delinquent horses, he had to break the silence.

"Is there something wrong?" he asked.

"We need to talk."

"Hell, I thought that's what we had been doing."

"I mean about important things."

"Oooh, I usually get further into a relationship before this conversation happens."

The horses let them approach and reclaim their bridles.

"Thanks for nothing," he told Sunflower when she nudged the front of his shirt.

"She's looking for peppermints. They both are." She stroked Pippi's nose.

"Well, they're not going to get any." Trent shook his head.

They walked the horses back to the barn. "So, are you breaking up with me?" he asked.

"What?" Kelly gawked at him. "No. Are we even together?"

"We could be. We should be. Don't you think?"

Taking a shuddering breath, Kelly led her horse into the stable and he followed. "Yeah, I think, but it's not that easy."

"Do you have a boyfriend?" Trent didn't think she would have let him kiss her like that if she was dating someone, but he couldn't think of anything else that could have been bothering her.

"It's not that." Kelly sighed. "I've got something to tell you and I'm not sure how to start."

"Just spit it out," he said, mildly. After taking off Sunflower's saddle and blanket, he helped Kelly take care of the horses and made sure they were secure in their stalls with food and water. But she didn't say anything until they were walking out of the barn.

"Come on back to the house for a minute, I want to grab my purse. I promise to rescue you from my dad. We'll talk over lunch."

"No worries," he said. "Whatever it is, we'll work it out."

"Yeah," she said softly with a trace of doubt in her voice.

He followed her into the ranch house. She led him into the living room where her father was sitting. Another woman and a child were there as well.

"Mom, this is Trent Campbell. Trent, my mother, Sarah Sullivan."

"Please don't get up. Nice to meet you, ma'am," he said, shaking her hand when she half rose out of her chair. "And who is this?" Trent used the back of the couch to settle himself down on one knee. His entire body locked and he bit down on a curse. He wasn't sure he'd be able to get back up.

The child looked like a fairy angel with wispy blonde

hair and deep blue eyes. She smiled and Trent was enchanted by the two little dimples that popped up in her cheeks.

"This is my daughter, Alissa."

He froze. This must have been what she wanted to tell him. "Howdy, ma'am," he managed to get out. Alissa giggled and ran to hide behind her grandfather's chair.

"I'm just going to grab my purse," Kelly said.

He heard her thunder up the stairs.

"So, Trent, I hear you're going to be the master of ceremonies at the rodeo," Sarah said.

"Yes, ma'am. I'm also going to be judging the mutton bustin'. Is that little lady going to be competing?" He winked at Alissa and she let out another stream of giggles again and ducked behind the chair again.

"No," Sarah said. "She's not old enough yet."

"Yes, she is," Frank said. "She'll love it."

"Oh? How old is she?"

Kelly must have flown back down the stairs, because suddenly she was at his elbow hoisting him to his feet. He saw stars and he swayed a bit, but he was up and apparently heading out the door at a fast clip.

"We've got to get going. See y'all later. Alissa, be good for MeMaw and PawPaw."

"Bye, Mommy," Alissa said, but she already engrossed in the cartoon on the television set.

"Bye! Nice meeting you." Trent let Kelly drag him out of the room.

Chapter Five

KELLY WASN'T READY for the big talk yet. She wasn't sure if she ever would be. She had to brace herself against the hurt of his indifference. Alissa was too great a kid to have to deal with that from her own father.

As it was, Alissa had started asking questions about who her father was and why wasn't he in their life. So far, Kelly had been able to deflect her by misdirection and changing the subject. That wasn't going to work for much longer. Maybe it was for the best that she'd be able to talk to Trent about it. However they decided to sling the story, it had to end with Alissa not feeling unwanted or unloved.

It was also hard to understand that Trent had no idea he was a father. She'd spent so much energy hating him for his indifference. Kelly had never even considered that he hadn't ever received her messages. What if he not only wanted Alissa, but wanted joint custody as well? The thought of not seeing her every day almost made Kelly physically ill. She had to get control of herself, of the situation. Forcing herself to take deep breaths, Kelly couldn't calm down. Jitters shook through her and she wanted to blurt out the truth instead of easing into it.

Once they were on their way, she couldn't hold back any longer. "What did you think of Alissa?"

"She's cute as a button, like her mama. Is her daddy in the picture?"

How could he have met Alissa and not seen his own eyes looking back at him?

"No," she said, her voice sounding breathless to her own ears.

"Then he's an idiot."

She groaned inwardly.

"You didn't have to worry about telling me about her. I love kids. I always wanted a big family."

"You did?" That just made it worse somehow.

"There was just never the time for a serious relationship." He frowned. "Seems like that's the story of my life. No time for anything but riding bulls." Trent looked at her. "I've got time now."

They pulled into the parking lot of the Last Stand Saloon, but she didn't make a move to get out of the car. Trent deserved to know, and Kelly deserved the consequences of not telling him about Alissa face-to-face all those years ago. Damn, she hated Last Stand. The worst moments of her life had happened in this town.

"What's the matter?" he said, gently rubbing her shoulder.

"Alissa is five years old."

She waited for him to do the math in his head. It took him a minute. Kelly didn't dare look at him.

"You had a boyfriend when we were together?" His voice

was strained.

"No."

"You had one right after, then." It was angry now. Accusatory.

"No." She forced herself to face him and the blazing blue temper in his eyes. "I called to tell you as soon as I found out I was pregnant. You never returned my calls or answered the messages I left."

"My phone was stolen," he gritted out. "You could have tried harder."

"I did. I called your manager."

He blinked. "Billy?"

"He didn't return my messages either. So, I called from a friend's phone, and when he answered, I told him I was six months pregnant. And that the child was yours. I demanded to speak with you. He said he'd give you the message."

"He didn't." Trent's jaw tightened.

"He didn't believe me that the child was yours. I called him a third time from New York."

"New York?"

"My father kicked me out when I wouldn't tell him who the father was."

"Kicked you out? Why didn't you tell him it was me?"

Kelly shook her head. "And be another buckle bunny trying to trick you into being a father? I didn't want you to be forced to acknowledge Alissa. And I didn't want to break my father's heart twice by making him see his favorite rodeo star in that light."

"I swear to you that I never knew." Despair tinged the

anger in his eyes.

It gutted her. "I know that now. But when I called Billy from New York, he said he gave you my message and you didn't want to be a father. You had other responsibilities. He offered me money."

"He what?" Shock shook through his voice.

"I told him where he could stick that money." She sighed. "I tried one last time. After the accident. She'd just been born. I wanted to send you pictures. I thought…" Kelly gave a shaky laugh and wiped away tears. "I thought even if you didn't want to be a part of our lives, seeing your daughter would have helped your recovery."

Trent closed his eyes. A tremor shook through him. His jaw was tight and his body seemed so tightly wound, she was afraid he was going to explode. "Are you sure she's mine?"

"What?" Kelly snapped. "Of course, I'm sure. You were the only man I was with."

"You said you were on the pill."

"I was. I…must have forgotten to take it that day. Or something. I don't know. Birth control wasn't anything I really had to pay attention to before. If I missed a day, big deal." Kelly gave a short humorless laugh. "Until it was a very big fucking deal." She heard the tears in her voice and tried to rein them back in. This was a long time coming and he deserved to ask these questions. Still, it stung that it felt as though he didn't believe her.

"You should have said something when the condom broke."

"At that point, I honestly thought we were protected. It

wasn't until the next morning when I saw there was an extra pill that I realized I hadn't taken it." Even then, she didn't think she could have gotten pregnant after one night. What were the odds? Let's just say she never went to Vegas after that. Not with her luck.

He sighed. "I grew up without a father. I never wanted a child of mine to have to suffer through that."

"She hasn't suffered."

"I should have been there. Just like my father should have been there for me."

"Why wasn't he?"

Trent gave a tight shrug. "Maybe he didn't want to be tied down with a kid. Maybe she never told him."

Kelly cringed. "Billy asked me if I was going to file a paternity suit. I said of course not. I didn't want anything from you. Then he said to take a hint and go away. So, I did."

"He had no right to do that." Trent's voice was quiet and menacing in the close space between them.

"I hadn't expected that we'd run into each other. I was going to avoid you at the rodeo."

"Why?"

"I didn't want to see you. I was mad at you."

"Mad at me? Would you have ever told me about Alissa?"

"If I saw you again. If you asked about her."

"It never occurred to you that I didn't get your messages?" His voice rose. "You thought I was the type of person who could turn my back on my own flesh and blood?"

"I didn't know what type of person you were," she argued. "We didn't have that type of relationship. Relationship? We had one night and a bunch of sexts. And then I never heard from you again, until you asked me to dance last night."

"I looked for you," he said, his hand over his face now. "I came back a few times to Last Stand."

"I was in New York. In exile." She gave a half laugh.

"Does she know I'm her father?" he whispered.

Kelly shook her head. "No."

"No? What did you tell her about her father?" He dropped his hand and stared at her incredulously.

"I said, he doesn't live with us and I changed the topic. She's been more insistent lately."

"What were you going to tell her?"

Kelly dropped her head back on the seat rest. "I was going to lie. I was going to make up a story. I thought about saying her father had been a soldier who died in a war. But that seemed disrespectful. Then I was going to say I was artificially inseminated, but that was too much to try to explain to a five-year-old."

"Why not the truth?"

"Because I thought the truth was her father didn't want her. And there was no way I was going to tell my baby girl that."

He stared out the window. Kelly could hear his ragged breaths.

"I'm trying to wrap my head around the fact that I could have lived my life without ever knowing I had a daughter. I'm not sure if I want to kill Billy or beat him within an inch of his life," Trent said between his teeth.

She flinched away at the violence in his tone. "I can't handle this right now." Reaching for the door handle, he stopped her with a firm grip on her arm.

"Let me go," she said, hearing the hysteria in her voice.

"Don't leave. Not yet. I'm not going to do anything like that. Truth be told, the old man could put me on my ass in one shot."

"That's not very comforting."

"I'm pissed, Kelly. I'm allowed to be pissed."

"At me?" she asked in a small voice.

He nodded. "I'm trying not to be. I believe you tried."

"Thanks," she said, tartly.

"Why didn't you come to see me? Why didn't you push your way through the crowd and grab me by the balls and tell me I was a bastard?"

"I didn't want to be humiliated. I didn't want you to call me a liar in front of everyone. I didn't want to be in the gossip columns and have my family's name dragged through the mud. I didn't want to force you to be a father. I didn't want that for Alissa. And I didn't want that for myself."

"Okay." He let out a big sigh. "Okay. I'm trying to think rationally here. I'm compartmentalizing my anger."

"You're what?"

"Something my therapist taught me. Anger isn't going to help the situation and if I let it, I'm going to be blinded by it. So, let's move on."

"Just like that?"

"Kelly, I'm trying here," he said between his teeth.

"Work with me."

"Fine. Where do you want to go from here?"

He was silent for a few moments and then he said, "I want my daughter to know I'm her father."

"Okay." She sagged in relief. "We need to come up with a story that she'll believe as to where you've been all her life." Some of the tension left his shoulders and the knot in her stomach started to slowly uncurl.

"I'd rather tell her the truth."

"She's too young for the truth."

"Well, I didn't mean all the sordid details. Just the bare bones of it."

Kelly looked him straight in the eye. "Do you want a relationship with her?"

"Yes."

Kelly let out a long breath. "What kind of relationship?"

"I'm her father."

"But she doesn't know you."

"She will," he said, and it sounded like a vow.

Kelly nodded. "Okay. We need to take this slow."

"Why? I almost died a few years ago. I don't take anything slow anymore because nothing is guaranteed."

"Because she is a five-year-old child and I don't want her confused or hurt."

"What will confuse or hurt her? Baby, I'm your daddy. I'm sorry I haven't been here, but I was hurt and in the hospital. Now, I'm here and you don't have to wonder about me ever again."

Okay, that would work. The pressure in Kelly's chest

eased some more. "That's a good way to tell her. But she's not my only concern. My father will flip his shit."

"I don't care. One less fan to gain a daughter? That's a bargain," he said.

"I care. His health isn't good. The ranch's finances have been a strain on him. Our relationship has just recovered. And he's been acting really strange lately, calling my sisters and me down here for one last time before he sold the ranch—which he had no intention of doing right away, as evidenced by your lease. I just need to know where I stand with him. I need to get centered here in Last Stand again."

"I can't believe he threw you out when you were pregnant."

"He was trying to force my hand."

"How did that work out for him?"

"He didn't talk to me for two years. It was only after his heart attack that he wanted to see me and Alissa. I'm afraid springing this on him suddenly will ruin our fragile truce, as well as upset him to the point he becomes irrational and does something he'll regret."

"So, her grandfather wasn't around for the first two years of her life, either?" Trent thumped the heel of his hand on the steering wheel.

"She had everyone else. She would have had him too, but he was too stubborn. Trent, all I'm asking is if we can take this slow?"

"I don't want to be your dirty little secret."

"You've been that for over five years."

He flinched.

"What's a few more months? Alissa and I will be living on the ranch while I get my business started. You can see her as often as you want. We'll tell her, together. And then we'll tell my father, together. But you have to do it on my schedule."

He blew out an angry sigh. "I don't see any point in waiting."

"I will get hurt, if you don't. Alissa will get hurt, if you don't. And quite frankly, I've been hurt enough." Kelly got out of the car. This time, he let her go. She slammed the door and stormed over to her car.

She'd leave Last Stand right now before she let Alissa feel her father's wrath or for one minute think she hadn't been wanted. She'd spare both of them the scene if her father decided to get ugly when he found out that Trent was Alissa's father. Kelly and Trent stared at each other through their windshields. Just as she was about to start up her car, she saw Trent curse and open his door.

Looking straight ahead, she rolled down her window as he approached.

"All right. We'll do it your way."

Tears pricked her eyes. "Thank you."

"I need some time to get my head on straight. Some space to process this."

"I'll give you all the time you want."

"It's not going to be that long. I just don't want you to think I'm ghosting you if I don't call you for a few days."

"That's not fucking fair."

He ran his hand through his hair. "You're right. I'm sorry. I guess what I'm trying to say is, what's your damned phone number?"

She took his phone and programmed it in.

Trent called her number.

When it rang, she raised her eyebrow at him. "Were you afraid I gave you a fake number?"

"No. Now you have my phone number again. I'm staying at the Bluebonnet Inn until after the rodeo, and then I'm moving out to the Three Sisters Ranch and living above the studio."

"You're going to live on the ranch?" She felt the world tilt a bit.

"I hadn't planned on it, but there's room upstairs for a modest apartment. You and Alissa will see me every day."

Kelly nodded. "Okay." This was going fast. Too fast. But she'd make it work.

"One other thing."

"Just one?" she asked wearily.

"The more comfortable we are with each other, the better this is going to be for Alissa."

"True."

"So, we should go out. On dates. Get to know each other."

She smirked. "Don't you think it's a little late to be courting me?"

"No, I don't. I'm not sure how this is all going to end up, but I'd like to take the time with you that I should have, all those years ago. I'm not the same guy I was back then. I've changed in good ways, but also in some bad ways."

Trent ran his hand through his hair. "I'm not going to have a lot of free time until after the rodeo, but maybe we can go out for a few drinks after?"

"I'm going to be asleep by the time the rodeo gets out." Kelly smiled. "I've changed in good and bad ways too."

"Then the day after the rodeo."

"I can do that," she said.

"Good." Trent leaned in through her window, surprising her with a quick kiss on her mouth.

It tingled and she blinked up at him in shock.

"I'll see you soon," he said and got back into his car and drove off.

It took her a few moments to realize she was staring off into space with a goofy smile on her face.

Chapter Six

TRENT DIDN'T REMEMBER driving back to the Bluebonnet Inn. He didn't remember knocking on Billy's door. But when Billy opened the door, he had to physically restrain himself from punching the older man in the face.

"What's gotten into you?" Billy asked, walking away from the door so Trent could come in.

"I just got back from the Sullivan ranch."

Billy frowned and sat down on the bed. The television was playing PBR reruns. "Something go wrong at the ranch? We've got an iron-clad contract. You can do whatever you want on that land for three years. Then, if they don't want to re-lease it to you, they have to compensate you for the improvements you've done on the place."

"It's not about the ranch. It's about a five-year-old girl named Alissa."

"I don't understand."

"Six years ago, I had an affair with Kelly Sullivan."

Billy cursed. "You never told me that."

"It's none of your damn business who I sleep with. She got pregnant. And had the child alone. Our child. You told her I knew and didn't want to be a father."

"Do you know how many women have claimed you're their baby daddy?"

"No, I damn well don't."

"Ten."

"Ten?" Trent swayed and held on to the doorframe.

"You want to come in or do you want to have this out in front of everyone in Last Stand?"

Trent closed the door in a daze and then the floor reached up to meet him as his leg gave out.

"Shit! You all right?" Billy came over and lifted him the way he had been taught by the nurses.

"I'm fine." Trent wanted to wave him off, but he literally didn't have the strength. Billy helped him hobble over to the bed.

"I'll get you some ice."

Trent stared up at the ceiling, hating himself. Hating everything.

When Billy got back with the ice, he poured it into the ice bucket liner and tied it into a knot. After helping him out of his pants, Billy arranged the ice pack under his hip. He went back for another one. Once his leg and hip were iced up, Trent sighed. "I want you to contact every one of them."

"Trent, you can't concentrate on this right now."

"I might have ten children."

"You don't."

"I have at least one. Why wouldn't there be others?"

"What makes you think this girl is yours?"

"Because her mother says so," Trent said between his teeth.

"Mothers lie."

"To what purpose?" Trent closed his eyes in frustration. "I'm not famous. I've got no money. Why would anyone lie that I'm the father of their baby?"

"Because you're a good man. You've got a future planned out. And you would take care of them, at the cost of your own self."

"I take responsibility for my actions. You're the one who taught me that," he said, glaring at him.

"Lord knows I tried my best, but you were a stubborn kid. What if they're not your actions, though?"

"What if they are? I did sleep with a lot of women when I was younger and full of myself. Ten women doesn't seem out of the question." Trent never thought his wild days would have consequences, which only went to show what an idiot he'd been.

"And you think you hit the bull's-eye each time? What are the odds of that?" Billy drawled.

"Do you still have the names of the women who claimed I was the father of their child?"

"No. Can you name ten women you might have impregnated?"

"Uh…" Trent screwed his face up while he thought. "I'm sure I could. If I still had my old phone, I'd definitely be able to." He wasn't good with names or numbers, but he'd had pictures of girls on his phone so when they'd call him, their images would come up. Unfortunately, he'd never backed any of that shit up and when his phone was stolen, he'd lost everything. He'd had been such a little jerk. Trent scrubbed his face with the heel of his hand. "I know first names. Some of them."

Billy shook his head. "You were never with anyone for more than a couple of nights, if that. You never mentioned any women to me. Besides, I raised you to use a rubber."

"I did," Trent groaned. "Mostly."

"Mostly? Jesus."

"The condom broke, but Kelly said she was on the pill."

"Well, the women usually called after you won a big purse or had been in the national news. I didn't take any of them seriously until the second or third call. Then I'd offer them some money to go away and keep their mouth shut."

"How much money?"

"A thousand dollars."

"A thousand dollars?" Trent's head hurt almost as much as his hip. "You paid ten thousand dollars to women who said they were carrying my child?"

"Give or take. If they took the money, they weren't really pregnant or it wasn't your kid."

"How do you figure?"

"Because a grand is chicken feed when faced with eighteen years of child support."

"Why did you pay them if they were lying?"

"Because it's cheaper to pay them off than worry about the bad press or legal fees."

So many questions. So many lies. "Why didn't you ever tell me?"

"You didn't need to know about the liars and the fakes. You had your career to concentrate on. I know a scam when

I see one. Some of them were repeat offenders."

"What do you mean?" He felt sick and useless, but he accepted the two Tylenol tablets Billy gave him and managed not to spill water all the way down his front.

"I mean they named a few other bull riders as their baby daddies as well, not figuring out that all the managers talk."

Trent was having a hard time wrapping his head around that. "All the women went away after you sent them a check?"

"Some came back for more. They wanted more money."

"And some told you to shove it up your ass."

"Not many did."

"Kelly Sullivan did. I want to know who else."

"When they tried to shake me down for more money or when they refused the money, I told them to send me a cheek swab from the baby and I'd get a DNA paternity test done. Guess what? No one ever did. Certainly not Kelly Sullivan."

"Do you remember her calling?" Trent grimaced as he tried to get comfortable. The ice numbed the pain, but the cold was starting to sting.

"No. I don't remember a Kelly Sullivan at all."

"You should have told me about the ones who refused the money."

"You didn't need the distractions. You didn't need to deal with the liars. That's my job."

"Kelly wasn't lying," Trent said.

"Then, have her send me a cheek swab from the kid and we'll swab your cheek and send it off to the lab for DNA testing."

"I believe her."

"I don't."

"It's not your business to believe it or not." Trent reminded himself that Billy was his oldest friend and, misguided or not, he'd always had his best interests at heart. Right now, though, it was tough not to hate him. It was tough not to hate himself. He should have been there for Kelly. Alissa should know who her father is. Of course, right now, Trent wasn't even sure who he was. He used to be a bull rider. He used to be a cocky kid who never turned down sex. What could he offer a daughter? He was just barely figuring things out for himself.

"It is if she's your biological daughter. We need to prove that, to protect your rights as a father. And if she's not your daughter, we need to protect your good name and your bank accounts. I'll send away for a kit."

"I'm not putting Alissa through that."

"It doesn't hurt. It's not a blood test. She doesn't even have to know what's going on."

"I said no."

"I'll handle it, if you want me to," Billy said.

"You're not going to do a damned thing. This could have all been solved five years ago."

"Five years ago, you were fighting for your life in a hospital room."

"Before that."

"Before that, you were preparing for the biggest ride of your life."

"This was more important. Kelly was more important. My daughter was more important." Trent yelled himself hoarse.

Billy waited until he was through and then waited a bit more. "What if she's not your daughter? What if Kelly Sullivan is lying?"

"Then why tell me? Why tell me now after all these years?"

"I don't know. Because she sees you as a threat to her father's ranch?"

"That's a little convenient, don't you think? I just happened to sleep with her five years ago, and she just happens to have a daughter the right age. You're the one who found the ranch, not me."

"Her father reached out to me."

"He did?" Was it possible that Kelly told her father and Frank Sullivan decided to take matters into his own hands? His gut said no. From what he saw this morning, subtlety wasn't in Frank's nature.

Would Trent be any different as a father? He already felt ridiculously protective of the little girl. He couldn't imagine reacting with any type of sense if some idiot was fool enough to hurt her. But then again, his own father never bothered with him. Unless, he never knew.

"Billy, I never knew my own father. It matters to me that no kid of mine ever has to feel that way. All I know about him is that he was a bullfighter."

"So your mother said."

"You don't believe it?"

Billy looked away. "I'm not going to talk about your mother. She was your mother and she did the best she could. And that's all I'm going to say about it."

"What if my dad never knew she had me? What if my father has spent the rest of his life not knowing he had a son?" Was it possible to track the man down after all these years to check? What would he even say to him? *It's been thirty years, but I'm the son you never knew you had.* Trent blew out a sigh. It was too late for him and his father. But it wasn't too late for Alissa.

"So, this is about you now?"

"No," he cried. "Wait. Yes, this is about me. Me and Kelly and Alissa."

"Trent, if this girl is your daughter, I will be the first one to apologize and do the right thing. But if she's not, you should get clear of the situation. I'll put a restraining order on Kelly Sullivan if I have to."

Trent shook his head. "No. You won't have to."

"I'll get the tests. You get the cheek swab."

"Fine. But after you get the tests, you're out of it. Don't talk to Kelly. Don't talk to Alissa and for all that's holy, don't talk to Frank Sullivan about this. And I want to know about the women who didn't take the money. I need to know if I have any more children I don't know about out there."

"Did the rubber break any other time?"

"No," Trent said hotly.

"Did you ever forget to wear one?"

"No."

"Then you don't have any little ones running around."

"I admit, it doesn't seem likely. But I'm not going to be able to sleep until you give me their names and I can check things out for myself."

"It's not like I kept records," Billy grumbled.

"Yes, you did. You keep records on everything. Let's start with the ones you paid off. I want to be thorough."

"You need to keep this on the down low or every buckle bunny with a kid about the right age will be clamoring for child support."

"Find the names and I'll take care of it."

"No. I'll hire an investigator. That way your name stays out of it."

"I still want to see the names."

"Don't get distracted."

"It's too damn late. Finding out that I'm a father is pretty damned distracting."

"You have a business to start. My business is making problems go away."

"A child isn't a problem. Not to me."

"I know, son." Billy sat down. "For what it's worth, I'm sorry. But I've seen it happen too many times with other riders that I managed. I didn't take them at all seriously."

"But you will now?"

"I'll consider it. I'll make some calls and do some follow-up."

"I want to know everything."

"All right." Billy got up, exasperated, and grabbed his laptop. He handed him the television remote. "I'm going to go downstairs for some peace and quiet. I'll be back before the ice melts."

"Thanks," Trent said, grudgingly.

Billy's face softened. "You're too trusting. After the life you had, I can't figure it out."

"You're too cynical," Trent countered, shifting the ice bags to another painful area.

"You know why I'm so cynical?"

"Because you're an ornery S.O.B.?"

"And the reason why is because people keep proving me right. I hope Kelly Sullivan isn't pulling a fast one to save her family's ranch from bankruptcy. But my gut tells me she is."

Trent closed his eyes and shook his head. "You're wrong."

"Guard your heart until you prove it, then."

That was the problem. Trent had a feeling he'd already fallen for both Kelly and Alissa.

Chapter Seven

A PILLOW LANDED on her face.

"Alissa, what have I told you about waking up Mommy?" Kelly muttered. She had hoped her parents would keep Alissa entertained so she could sleep past nine a.m. for the first time in five years.

The bed dipped as someone heavier than Alissa sat next to her and walloped Kelly again with a pillow.

"That's it." Grabbing her pillow, Kelly came up swinging. "Janice!" she said, not slowing the arc of the pillow. "When did you get in?" She landed a pillow strike upside her younger sister's head.

Janice looked like an evil librarian, with her cat's-eye glasses and short dark blonde hair. But she swung a pillow like Babe Ruth. Janice "the smart one" took pride in doing crossword puzzles with a pen and playing dirty, like ambushing her sleeping sister.

"I came in late last night." Janice got off the bed and shook the pillow at her threateningly. "Dad forced Nate to come get me because he didn't want me to take an Uber."

Janice was freshly showered and smelled like her favorite lilac soap. She was wearing a wrinkle-free suit jacket and

101

slacks with a red shell underneath it. Her hair looked recently cut short. It was curling a bit around her temples.

"You got a job interview?" Kelly said groggily.

"We have an interview."

"We do?"

"With Kendrick Moore at the bank. He's reviewing both of our loan applications today. Two birds, one stone. That type of thing."

Kelly yawned so hard, her jaw cracked.

"Come on and get dressed. We have to meet him in a little over an hour."

"Why so early?"

"I don't know what you mean. I've been up since five."

Kelly threw the pillow at her sister's retreating back.

It was just like Janice to have arranged for a meeting with the bank on the morning after she arrived. After reluctantly rolling out of bed, Kelly shuffled into the bathroom to get ready. She had never applied for a loan before, but it couldn't be too hard. The collateral thing was going to be a problem. She didn't own anything, but she had a steady job and had never been late on her bills, so Kelly hoped it was just going to be a formality. After seeing Trent's barn and studio, she was eager to have her area set up so she could start taking promotional shots.

Stretching, Kelly got into the shower. She was glad Janice was here—one more missing piece of her family snapping back into place. As she lathered up, she was surprised that she felt lighter and happier than she had in a while. Not only did she feel less alone with Janice here as a buffer between her and her parents, but she couldn't deny she was also relieved that Trent knew about Alissa.

One down, two to go. She thought Alissa would handle it well. She took everything in stride and nothing seemed to affect her for very long. Her father on the other hand, well, he had to be handled with kid gloves. They would have to use Billy King as a scapegoat, because he was the reason Trent hadn't known he was a father until last night. She only hoped her father wouldn't go after Billy with a shotgun. Frank's temper was legendary.

Janice had been dating a guy who treated her like hell. One night, she came back with a red mark on her face and bruises on her arm. The next day, her mother'd had to bail her father out of jail and they had to pay for damages to the guy's car. Of course, a few days later, when her parents had an alibi, the guy got mugged and beaten within an inch of his life. All the ranch hands said Nate had been in the barn with them, but Kelly always had her doubts about that, especially since he wore gloves for the next few days. The guy left town right after that. Good riddance. But it always made Kelly a little wary about what her father could be trusted to know.

It had been so different living with her aunt. There was no walking on eggshells or shouting. She missed that peaceful existence, but she couldn't deny that the ranch made her blood stir. All she wanted to do was go riding, and she wanted to share that joy with Alissa too. Kelly got dressed in a flowing skirt and a peasant blouse, and then went downstairs to see what her daughter was up to. She was playing checkers with her grandfather and Kelly had a moment to study both of them.

Her father looked tired. He'd lost weight since the last time they were down here, which probably elated his heart surgeon, but Kelly wasn't used to seeing her dad so gaunt. At least, he wasn't smoking anymore. But his fingers trembled slightly when he moved the checker piece. He couldn't take his eyes off his granddaughter, and he beamed at her with pride.

Kelly had loved playing chess with him when she was younger. It was one of the few times he was patient, when he was showing her how to play a game, or shoot a rifle, or ride a horse. Kelly often thought he would have been a good teacher if the ranching bug hadn't hit him. Alissa made a mistake and Kelly would have jumped her piece and gone for the win, but her father pretended he didn't see it.

"You're a softy," she murmured.

Alissa had dressed herself this morning, meaning she was wearing a cowboy hat and one of Kelly's band T-shirts. A tutu cinched the shirt, making it a dress. New cowboy boots that looked like something Janice would have bought topped off the look. She was eating a bowl of strawberries and concentrating so hard on the game, she jumped when Kelly pressed a kiss on her cheek.

"Good morning, sunshine," she said, stealing a piece of fruit.

"PawPaw is winning."

"That happens." Kelly glanced at her father. "Are you and Mom okay watching her while Janice and I hit the bank?

Or should we take her with us?"

"I want to stay," Alissa said. "MeMaw is going to let me play with the kittens again."

"Go out with your sister," her father said. "Alissa doesn't need to sit in a bank all day when she could be having fun outside in the country. She's too used to being cooped up in that big city of yours."

"Yeah," Alissa said, stuffing two strawberries in her mouth. Her lips and fingers were already stained with berry juice.

"We weren't going to be gone all day, but we could be," Kelly said wryly.

"Suit yourselves."

Kelly looked him over in concern, but he seemed fine. She wasn't used to him being at the table at this time in the morning or being so agreeable. He would have normally been on his horse with Nate at this time of day.

"Hurry up," Janice called from the porch.

Pouring herself a coffee and snagging a muffin, Kelly joined Janice on the porch swing. Their mother was weeding the garden and waved at her when she sat down next to her sister.

"We're taking your car," Janice said.

"Nate can't drive us to the bank?" she teased, knowing Nate was with the cattle.

She snorted. "It was bad enough he had to pick me up last night. He barely said two words to me. He wouldn't tell me what the buildings up by the road were. Dad said I had to wait for Emily."

Placing her coffee mug down, Kelly rummaged through her purse for the rental car keys. "Here, you drive so I can eat breakfast on the way." She tossed her sister the keys. "When *is* Emily going to get here?"

"Not until next week. She's pretty upset she's going to miss the rodeo. Did you see who's the master of ceremonies?" Janice got up and dusted off her skirt before heading to the car.

"Yes." Kelly smirked, getting in the car and buckling in.

"I wonder if he's still as fine as he used to be."

"He is."

"Really?" Janice gave her the side eye as they pulled out of the driveway.

Kelly finished her muffin, timing her next sentences just right. She took a long sip of coffee to wash it down... And... Now... "Dad leased him the property you saw. These are his buildings. That's his soon-to-be-open bull-riding school." She pointed as they were passing it.

"What?" Janice slammed on the brakes.

Kelly just managed not to slosh coffee on her skirt.

Putting the car in park, Janice flew out the door and hurried over to the buildings. Kelly followed more slowly. "I don't think we're supposed to be here."

Trent poked his head out from the door of the studio as they got closer. Janice halted in shock and Kelly almost plowed into the back of her.

"Hey," he said, walking up to Kelly. "Didn't expect to see you here so early." And then to her mortification, he brushed a quick kiss over her lips.

Little flutters of pleasure jingled down her spine and she wished she had the guts to ask him to kiss her like he meant it.

Janice made a strangled gurgle.

"I'm Trent Campbell." He turned to her and held out his hand.

When Janice blinked rapidly at him and her mouth made fish movements, Kelly jumped in. "This is my sister, Janice."

Janice recovered her wits enough to shake his hand.

"Nice to meet you," he said. "Kelly tells me you're going to build a women's retreat."

"She did?" Janice said, her eyes wide. "I am. I thought my father was selling the ranch. Did you buy it?"

"No," Trent said. "I just leased a little bit of it. We're testing out a bull-riding school here." He gestured around. "I can option for multiple years at the end of the lease or cut bait if the school tanks. Can I give you the tour?"

Janice slumped. "I'd love to see it, but we can't. We're heading out to the bank."

"Later then. Come on by anytime." He paused and then looked right at Kelly. "Bring Alissa too. I have a T-shirt that would fit her with the school's logo on it."

Now it was Kelly's turn to sputter. "We'll see," she managed to say.

Trent watched them get back into the car and gave them a quick wave before going back into the building.

"What the hell was that all about?" Janice asked, her eyes wide.

"You heard him. He's paying rent. That's Dad's big secret. He was waiting for Emily to get here before he told us. He's not planning on selling right away. He lied to us to get us to come down here." Kelly took a sip of her coffee. "I'm kinda pissed about that. It's manipulative."

"The hell with that right now. Trent Campbell kissed you. And he kissed you like it wasn't the first time."

Kelly felt her cheeks flush hot. "We're seeing each other in a very casual, getting to know you sort of way."

"When did this happen? You didn't say a word."

"It happened really recently." Kelly felt a little guilty at the white lie, but she was also waiting for Emily to come home before spilling her secret.

"You've only been in town a few days. You don't waste time. I guess it's because you've had a crush on him forever." Janice shook her head in disbelief. "A bull-riding school, huh? Do you think there will be any takers?"

"With his name behind it? You bet. He's going to be busy."

"He's going to need a parking lot," Janice muttered.

"You're going to need a parking lot too."

"Dad's not going to like all the asphalt. Neither is Nate."

"Tell me about it," Kelly said. "But we can't have our guests driving off road to get to us. I'm going to need your help to sweeten them up to the idea. How long are you here for?" Kelly asked.

Janice made a face. "I'm here for the time being. I'm going to give notice at my job. I'm using up my vacation now, and I'll still have to fly back and forth to be at a few more dressage shows. But by the end of the year, I'll be here full-time."

"Do you think that's wise?"

"The women's retreat is my idea. I need to be here."

"But what if this doesn't work? What if next year or the year after, Dad goes through with his threat and sells the ranch? Where will you go?"

"Wherever I want. Every town needs a veterinarian."

"Will your old job take you back?" Kelly asked.

"Maybe, but it was time to move on. And who knows, maybe the new owners of the ranch would let me keep my retreat."

"Wouldn't that be something? Dad and Mom clear out and we're still here."

"I can't imagine them not being here," Janice said. "It's one of the reasons we all came rushing back."

"For nothing." Kelly crossed her arms in front of her. "He's got another couple of years before he was planning to sell. He guilted all of us into turning our lives upside down to come back here. I'm so pissed at him for that. He could have been straight with us instead of playing on our emotions."

"I don't know," Janice said. "Sure, he could have done it less dramatically. But this way, he's giving us time to build the ranch back up. Two years of rent with Trent and Donovan—"

"And us."

"And us. It could make all the difference. If he was planning on selling by the end of the year, there's no way we could have saved the ranch."

Kelly didn't want to let logic take away her righteous anger. "I still say he could have treated us like adults for once in our lives and told it to us straight."

"It was lucky that all of us were ready for a new direction. I like to think that this was his way of pushing us to make a decision that we wanted to make."

"I didn't want to come here," Kelly argued. "I liked New York."

"You liked living in a cramped apartment with Aunt Candace?"

"We were saving up to get our own apartment," Kelly said defensively.

"Would that double as your photography studio?"

"Maybe," she muttered.

"This is a better opportunity," Janice said, gently.

"It is if he doesn't kick me out again."

"And that's why you're really mad."

Kelly couldn't argue.

"If you have a contract, he can't kick you out."

"He's not going to give me a contract."

"Don't worry," Janice said. "I'm positive it will be a condition of the bank loan."

"You think?"

"Yup. Make the bank the bad guy and get the legal paperwork and Dad won't be able to kick you out until the lease is up. And by that time, you'll have a good idea how everything stands."

How everything stands—including Trent.

Kelly nodded. "It's a good thing you're the smart one."

"Shut up," Janice said, annoyance making her voice hard. "You are not a dumb blonde."

"And you are not the ugly duckling."

If Emily was here, she would have piped up that at least they weren't "the baby."

They joked about the monikers now, but growing up, it had hurt. She knew she wasn't stupid and Janice knew she wasn't ugly. But sometimes they wondered if their father knew that.

"Anyway, once things settle down with the bank, Nate is lending me the horse trailer so I can drive back and pick up Black Dahlia and Synergy. I can put Syn out to stud and keep my head above water until I'm all set up."

Black Dahlia was an Andalusian who'd won a few FEI competitions, but had her own ideas on when and where she wanted to perform. Janice spoiled her like crazy, having raised her since she was a foal. Synergy was a racehorse who'd never won a race, but his bloodlines were impeccable.

"Is that all you're bringing back?" Kelly asked, knowing her sister.

"Of course not. I've got the dogs to take home with me as well. They're at Jolene's right now."

Jolene was her best friend in Kentucky. "How many dogs are we up to now?"

"Six."

"Six?" Kelly asked, incredulously.

"It was more, but we lost Buck and Lou to cancer."

"I'm sorry," Kelly said. She had liked the beagles.

"Yeah, me too. I wish I could have done more for them."

"You made their last few years comfortable. Sometimes, that's all you can do." Kelly had a terrible thought that her father might be on his last years as well. Maybe that was why he went for all the dramatics and told them he was selling the ranch.

"Oh, I examined the kittens. They don't have any worms or any colds. Alissa should be fine to play with them."

Janice found out a long time ago that she was too soft to work on a ranch where the animals were not pets. She was a good livestock doctor, but her heart was in helping domesticated house pets instead of trail horses and sick cattle. However, she'd been horse crazy since she was a little girl. She recommended Emily buy Sunflower and had hand-picked Pippi for Kelly. While Kelly and Emily had been barrel racers, Janice had studied English equestrian events and made their father build her a dressage ring to practice in.

"I don't think we could have stopped Alissa even if they weren't. She was smuggling them into the house in her pockets," Kelly said, wondering how she was going to convince her parents to let them keep the orange tabby that they'd both fallen in love with as a pet.

Janice smiled and pulled into the Last Stand Bank's parking lot. "I'm feeling really good about this."

The three of them had sent in their plans to Kenny along with the online application. Emily would have to come in and do her interview separately, but Kelly would go with her if she needed some support. She had to admit, it was a little scary to ask for money.

Kenny came out and gave them both big hugs. He hadn't changed since high school. He had an infectious grin and looked like a grown-up version of Howdy Doody. After a few moments of small talk, Kenny said, "Kelly, let's start with you."

"The oldest always goes first," Janice said in mock exasperation and took a seat in the lobby with a cup of coffee.

When the door closed behind them, Kelly's nerves fluttered a bit. Kenny suddenly became all business. "I looked over your application and your income statements and I was impressed. How did you manage to pay off your student loans so quickly?"

"I work for my aunt in New York and business was good. It helped that Alissa and I stay with her rent free, so I could manage my debt and build up some savings."

He tapped a pen on his desk. "The savings aren't quite where we'd like them to be."

Kelly nodded. "I know. It seems every time I started making headway on that, an emergency would happen."

"Ain't that always the way. I've read what you wrote, but I want you to walk me through your plans. Your daddy agreed to rent you an acre of land."

"Yes." Kelly cleared her dry throat. "I'm a professional photographer and I want to build a small portrait studio and gallery for my pictures. I have fantastic references from several schools and brides I've worked with."

Kenny nodded encouragingly. "So the loan would be for the building and supplies."

"And rent."

He frowned. "That's not quite what we'd like to see. Your business's profit should be making the money to pay rent. Otherwise, once the loan runs out…" He shrugged.

"I know," she said. "My father has signed on a few other tenants as well."

"Yes, Mr. Link and Mr. Campbell. That must be exciting to have all that activity."

"Yes, and all the businesses will complement each other. I could do trophy photographs for the hunters." That made her a little uneasy, but she knew she could do a professional job. "And for Trent's school, I could do student portraits or action shots." She straightened up in her chair. "I'll be taking candids at the rodeo and selling them to the local papers and posting them online. I have a good marketing plan and I know the business will be successful. Meanwhile, I'm still working jobs for my aunt back in New York as a means to pay the bills until I get established."

He sighed. "Look, I'm going to come right out and say this—your aunt doesn't pay you a salary."

"That's right. I work on commission."

"The bank doesn't like not seeing a regular paycheck."

Kelly leaned forward in her chair. "Oh, but the work is steady. I even have backlog." Especially this week. She needed to hunker down and Photoshop the Winston wedding party, otherwise Candace was going to call her up, hollering for blood.

He shuffled through some of the paperwork. "Your last three months have been erratic. Some weeks much less than others."

"But if you look at the last three years, you can see that my income has been pretty even."

"I'm afraid that's not strong enough for the loan. I'm sorry."

"You're turning me down?" Fear and that old familiar feeling of shame coursed through her.

"This is the bad part of my job. Turning down good people for loans."

"But this loan would let me build up a business. I would be turning a profit quickly. Didn't you see the business plan I submitted?" Kelly forced herself to sound calm and professional, but inside she was shaking apart. She had wanted to go back to her father with a rental agreement on her terms, not with her tail between her legs.

"We did take that into account, but I think you're basing the business on New York interests. The bank felt it was a risky investment for a town as small as Last Stand."

"I see." Kelly swallowed hard. "Thank you for your time."

She shook his hand and walked back out into the lobby. Refusing to meet Janice's gaze, she poured herself a cup of coffee—might as well get something out of the bank today. Wandering over to the lobby, she sank down in her chair and tried to regroup as her sister went in for her meeting.

She could go back to New York. The ranch wasn't in any immediate danger. But Trent had complicated things. Now that he was staying in Last Stand, would he want joint custody of Alissa? Kelly almost choked on her coffee. She couldn't imagine being without Alissa for a weekend, not to mention a few weeks or months out of the year. That made her hands shake so much, she almost spilled the coffee. Placing it down on the side table, she crossed her arms over her chest, hugging herself.

She wasn't leaving her daughter. Even if her parents were right down the road from Trent, she wouldn't be able to sleep in New York if Alissa wasn't with her. Which meant, she was staying in Last Stand. She would have to face her father every day, and instead of her helping him out of a jam, she would be reliant on him.

Kelly stood up and paced. Of course, had her father not tricked her into riding to his rescue, they could have all happily gone on with their lives, not knowing the truth. And yet, she couldn't regret it. It was a relief to know Trent hadn't ghosted her. It healed places she didn't know were wounded.

So much for her photo studio, though. Disappointment fluttered through her. Kelly hadn't realized how much she wanted her own business until the prospect was gone. She'd stick around and help her sisters, if they didn't get turned down as well. And if that happened, their only chance at saving the ranch was the rent money that Trent and Donovan were bringing in. From what Mom said, that money would buy time, but it wouldn't solve the problem.

The worst part of this was going back to her father a failure. The coffee churned in her stomach. She had wanted to impress him. She wanted to shine for him again. She wanted to be successful so when she had to disappoint him again by revealing Trent as Alissa's father, it would be all right because she had helped save the ranch.

Janice came out about a half hour later, looking as dazed as Kelly had felt.

"What happened?" Kelly crossed the lobby to get to her.

"Let's grab some pie," Janice said with a fake smile. She wouldn't meet her eyes.

Oh, that bad. Pie before lunch was medicinal and the calories didn't count. They hit the Last Stand pie shop and slid into a booth. Janice ordered a slice of apple pie with vanilla ice cream, but Kelly was all in with chocolate fudge pie with real whipped cream.

"So, you got turned down too."

"No." Janice sighed. "But I almost wish I had."

"Why?" Kelly asked, happy for her sister, but miserable for herself. She was also worried about Emily. Unless Emily could call in some favors, it didn't look good for her either. As far as she knew, Emily didn't even have a decent-paying job.

"I didn't tell the bank I was planning to give notice to my job in Kentucky, and I had to put my horses up for collateral."

Kelly dropped the fork she had been about to dig into the pie. "You can't do that."

"It's done. It's a good motivation to get things up and running so I don't miss a payment. I've got some savings, but they're not going to last long."

"I can help a bit. I've got a few credit cards to max."

"You're going to be busy with your own project."

"No. Didn't you hear me? I got turned down. I don't

have enough on my cards to go forward without the loan." Kelly stared down at her plate. Not even chocolate could make her feel better. It stung that she was going to have to return to her father with the hint of shame again.

Janice ate a few bites of pie. "It's not like you to give up like this."

"I'm not giving up. I said I'd help you."

"We need to think about what we need. I think we should combine our savings and credit cards and with that and the loan, we can build both. My women's retreat can share a parking lot and some facilities with your photo studio. I could use your photos as decoration and sell them in the gift shop. Meanwhile, we could have you on trail rides to take candid pictures. I know it's not exactly what you wanted, but I can add a photo studio and shop into the retreat house. It'll be tiny," she said apologetically.

Kelly's head whipped up. "No, it'll be perfect. The only thing is I won't be paying Dad rent."

"But I will be. I know we wanted to give him two income streams, but I'll make sure the rent is high enough that it will be as close as possible to what the two of us would be paying him."

"This could work," Kelly said, getting excited again.

"We should coordinate with Emily," Janice added. "Maybe there are nature lovers or kids who'd like to get their pictures taken."

"Do you think Donovan Link would hire me for trophy portraits?"

Janice made a face. "I don't think that's going to work."

"Why not?"

"Emily will flip her shit if you're taking a picture of Bambi hanging from a tree with a yahoo and his shotgun grinning into the camera. I think you'd be better off asking Trent if he'd pose for a few pictures. Without his shirt on."

"Janice," Kelly warned.

"What? A girl can dream, right?"

"Well, wake up. He's taken."

"Is he?" Janice smiled slyly.

"I could do a ranch hand catalog shoot. Do you think I could get Nate to strip down and pose with Sunflower and Pippi?"

"I think you'd have a better chance getting Dad to do it," she said dryly. "Seriously, though. Trent's students are going to want some professional pictures with him and their parents are definitely going to eat up any candids you take. You need to wow everyone with your rodeo shots, though."

"I plan to. What are you going to work on?"

"The retreat center. It's going to be rustic as hell. The guests can't be expecting a five-star spa and resort. It's camping and survival skills. I'm going to need you to tell a story with your pictures for the brochure and the website." Janice stabbed at her pie with a little more gusto.

"You got it. I won't let you lose Synergy and Black Dahlia." Kelly reached her hand over and clutched her sister's. "I think this is going to work."

"Of course, it's going to work. We're Sullivans. We don't give up."

Chapter Eight

TRENT WAS INSTALLING a television on the mounting frame inside the studio when he heard a trailer pull up. By the time he was able to secure the TV onto the base, there was a lot of commotion outside. After stepping down from the ladder, Trent went outside to see what the ruckus was all about. Frank Sullivan and his granddaughter—*his* daughter—were standing outside of the pen, looking at a sheep.

Trent didn't own a sheep.

Frank turned around as they approached. "I want you to teach my little girl, here, how to ride a sheep for the mutton-busting event."

Trent wasn't prepared for that. He leaned up against the pen and said, "She needs equipment. I don't have anything in stock yet for the little ones."

"Got it covered." Frank went into the truck and came back with rope, a protective chest vest, gloves, and a helmet. "We went shopping in the city. The rigging fits the sheep. I already checked."

"You did, huh?"

"You got the chute all prepared. What do you say?"

Hunkering down to Alissa's level, Trent asked her,

"What do you think?"

Her eyes were blue and sparkling. He had a lump in his throat, and he was not expecting the wave of emotion that flooded over him. So, this was love at first sight. Alissa was his daughter. Did he want to have this time with her? Hell yeah.

"She nodded vigorously, her blonde curls bouncing up and down.

"Can she ride a pony?" he asked Frank, as he got up.

"She's been on one with me or Nate leading her."

"It's going to be a little like that at first," he said to her. "But before we put you on top of the sheep, we're going to have to go over the basics and talk about safety. That might be a little boring."

"I promised her pink chaps with leather fringes. She'll sit through anything," Frank drawled.

She would look adorable in that outfit. "I hadn't thought about doing wool-riding lessons, but why not? I'm game if you are."

Alissa nodded again, and slipped her hand into his. He lost another piece of his heart.

"Okay," he said, leading her into the studio. "We're going to practice how to fall, because you're probably going to fall."

"Will it hurt?" she asked with a little wobble in her voice.

He started to get second thoughts. "Where did you get the sheep from?" he asked Frank.

"I bought it. It's been used in the rodeo before. It's a good first ride. It's yours, by the way."

"Mine?"

"What am I going to use a sheep for?" Frank said. "Keep it for the school. For the little ones."

"Her name is Flower," Alissa said. "And I love her."

Well, that was that. "All right. Thank you. I'll make Flower a home here."

Trent didn't have a curriculum set up for mutton busting, but he did his best. He gave Alissa the T-shirt he was saving for her that had his bull-riding school logo on it. She immediately put it on. Then, they went over the equipment and how important it was to take care of it. After that, he fished around for a few videos off YouTube and had her watch them on his phone.

"Just get on with it already," Frank said, exasperated. "Stick her on the back of the sheep and let's go."

"Patience," Trent admonished, keeping the edge out of his voice. The old man was pushy, but he had his heart in the right place. It made him wonder what his father would have been like. Would he have wanted Trent to follow in his footsteps? Would he have been proud when he became a professional bull rider instead? Had Trent ever met him and neither of them knew they were father and son? Maybe a DNA test would show him who his father was. Or at least a match. But he couldn't think about that right now. Not when his own flesh and blood was sitting next to him. "You want her to love this, right?"

"She'll love it."

"She'll love it, if she's prepared."

Next, they practiced how to fall and to tuck and roll

away from the hooves.

"It's not a bull, for Pete's sake. The sheep will probably stop running before she falls off."

"Probably," Trent said, mildly.

Then they worked on gripping the rope and he had her stand on a riser while he gently pushed her to see how she would keep her balance. Alissa was a sweetheart, with a fierce scowl and a determination that he was enchanted with. He wished he knew her mother better than one night, a handful of texts and a few stolen kisses. Trent was going to remedy that because if she was even half as amazing as her daughter, Trent was going to make sure Kelly Sullivan was all his.

"All right, I think you're ready to try the sheep."

"Well it's about damn time," Frank said, tiredly. He looked drawn and snappish and was having a hard time getting up from his chair. He accepted an arm up from Trent.

"You okay?" Trent asked.

"I'll live," Frank said grimly.

Trent rounded up Flower and got her ready for a ride. It seemed surreal to be standing in the chute, but aside from having his foot stepped on, he wasn't in danger. Frank lifted Alissa and handed her to him. For a moment, she clung to Trent and his heart flipped over. He settled her on the back of the sheep.

"Are you scared?" he asked.

She nodded.

"I was too the first time I did this. But those butterflies in your stomach are worth it for the thrill."

"What if I fall?" she asked.

"You'll get banged up a bit. Maybe get dirt in your mouth, if you have it open. But your grandpa and I will be right there to pick you up."

"Okay," she said.

"Now, remember, hold on tight. Dig your feet in and put your toes out."

She smiled.

Frank had made his way to the front of the chute.

"All right, then. Give your gate man the nod when you're ready."

She did.

Swinging the gate open, Frank jogged into the center of the paddock anticipating a mad dash. The sheep trotted out, the bell attached to the harness startling it. Alissa held on like a champ and Trent ran alongside it. Sure enough, it stopped running before she could fall off and he swooped her up and twirled her around.

"You did it!" he said.

"Again!" she cheered.

"What the hell is going on here?" Kelly asked from outside of the paddock.

"I'm mutton bustin', Mommy." Alissa wiggled down and ran to her mother. "I did great."

"Don't fuss over the child," Frank said, leading the sheep back into the chute.

"She's my child to fuss over." But then Kelly met Trent's eyes and looked away.

"She was perfectly safe," Trent said. "I made sure she was

prepared."

"Yup, we did drills and watched videos," Alissa said, climbing up the rails of the paddock. "I didn't get a chance to fall. And we practiced that."

"You did?" Kelly asked faintly.

"Can I go again?"

Trent felt badly. "I'm sorry. Your father came here with all the gear and the sheep. I assumed you knew about it."

"Not only did I not know about it, I also told him I didn't want her to compete this year."

"PawPaw is going to get me pink fringed chaps." Alissa climbed over and went around to the studio.

"And now I'll be the bad guy for saying no." Kelly shook her head.

"It's safe," Trent said. "Just go and help her on the sheep. Your dad will open the gate and I'll keep watch in the pen. The sheep is a real pro."

"All right," she said, dejected.

"How did the bank go?" he called after her.

"I'll tell you later."

Janice came up to the fence. "This looks like fun. Too bad I'm in my good clothes."

"Go change and come back," Trent suggested.

"Nah, I'll just watch."

Kelly appeared holding Alissa's hand. She lowered her on the sheep. "Hold on tight."

Alissa nodded like a pro and Frank opened the gate. This time the sheep ran fast and Alissa slipped under him, still holding on.

"Let go," Trent called, sprinting over to her.

She covered and rolled and was on her knees by the time he scooped her up.

"Alissa?" Kelly called.

"I'm okay." She waved. "I didn't get dirt in my mouth. Let's do it again!"

They set her up a few more times, but then the sheep was getting tired. "All right, Flower needs a break," Trent said.

"And you need a bath," Kelly said to her daughter.

"I want to ride a bull next."

"No," all the adults said at the same time.

Alissa pouted and crossed her arms over her chest.

"Mutton busters don't pout," Trent said.

"That wasn't in the rules," Alissa countered.

Trent blinked at her, momentarily lost for words. "Well, it should have been."

"I'll bathe her," Janice said to Kelly. "You're dressed all nice. Why don't you take Trent out to lunch? I'll catch a ride back with Dad."

"I wouldn't say no," Trent said.

"All right," Kelly agreed.

Trent wasn't sure he trusted the look in her eyes. She still seemed a little steamed. But he was eager to spend some time with her and hear all about Alissa.

"Helluva time, Trent. Thank you." Frank clapped him on the shoulder.

"I've got a video of some of the rides," Janice said. She showed her phone to Alissa. "If it's all right with the two of you, I can post it on YouTube and you can use it for promotion for your school."

"It's all right by me." He looked at Kelly.

"Let me think about it," she said, taking her keys back from Janice.

"Okay. Have fun you two." Janice smiled and helped Alissa get into Frank's truck.

"She did great," Trent said as they watched them drive back toward the house. "Has she always been so fearless?"

"No, but her grandfather's approval works magic. Ask me how I know."

"I'm sorry, I should have called to check with you."

"It's okay. I'm not annoyed with you."

"Well, that's good at least. She did great. She's going to be a cowgirl."

"I hope so."

"What do you mean?"

"My father always does shit like that. He does what he wants and to hell with everyone else. He's a master manipulator. I bet he buttered you up so you couldn't say no."

"He bought me a sheep and Alissa some state-of-the art gear. I wish I'd had that stuff when I was a kid. Of course, I probably would have done even more dangerous stuff if I had."

"That sounds like something he would do."

They got in the car.

"Where to?" Trent asked.

"We could go to Draeger's Peach House," Kelly suggested.

"I can practically taste the peach pie. So, is this our official first date?" Trent asked as they pulled out of the ranch and onto the road.

"I guess it is," she said with a small smile. "I wish we could be celebrating, but I didn't get the loan."

"I'm sorry to hear that."

"Me too. I thought it was back to New York for us."

Trent tensed up.

"It makes things more difficult, but my sister is going to share her loan money and I think we can help each other become profitable. And if by some miracle Emily is approved, we'll be in decent shape."

"Good. Let me know if I can help." Some of the tension eased. There was time to see if he and Kelly could have a relationship that went beyond just being Alissa's parents. He'd have time to get to know his daughter, at the very least, and he wanted to be in her life. And he'd have a hard time doing that if she lived in New York.

He didn't want to have to get a lawyer and demand it, though. Of course to do that, he had to prove she was his. He considered bringing up the cheek swab, but didn't want to ruin this time they had. It could keep for a few more weeks.

"Funny you should offer," Kelly said. "What do you think about having me sell my services as a photographer to your students?"

"I don't have any yet."

"You will," she said. "And they're going to want pictures of them riding their first bull."

"I only have a sheep."

"I mean eventually.

Trent shrugged. "Sure."

"Great, we can talk about that later. My head is swimming from having to pivot back and forth this morning. At first, I thought I was going to get the loan easily. Then when it was denied, I figured I was going back to New York. Then I decided to stay. It wasn't an easy decision. Part of me thinks I should go back home."

He frowned. He wasn't ready to say goodbye to either of them yet.

"But then Janice came through and we're going ahead with everything, just on a different time schedule and budget." She snapped her fingers. "That reminds me. I need to find a gazebo, stat, and have it set up. I'm going to have to modify my original plans from the gorgeous thirteen-thousand-dollar Victorian gazebo to something more budget-friendly."

"Thirteen thousand dollars?" That seemed like a lot of money to him.

"I may have to go to Home Depot and get one for three grand instead, and hold off on the better one until I get some brides who want to use it for their engagement or wedding shots."

The restaurant was busy with the lunch crowd, but they were able to get a table inside. Trent was glad for the air-conditioning and the soft booth. His leg still gave him a bit of a twinge, but the ice last night had helped. He wound up falling asleep in Billy's room, so Billy had bunked down in his.

"How did you get to the ranch?" Kelly asked after they placed their orders. "I didn't see a car."

He could practically taste the steak sandwich. He hadn't eaten anything since the kolaches this morning. He was addicted to the Czech pastries the Bluebonnet Inn served. "Billy dropped me off. I need to look into getting a vehicle, but it's not a priority."

"Well, you heard my priority. Mission gazebo. What's your priority?"

"You," he said. "And Alissa."

She looked at him in shock.

"It occurred to me while I was spending time with my daughter, that I've spent more time with her than I have with you and that seems all sorts of wrong." Trent reached over and held her hand.

Kelly glanced around the restaurant. "People will see."

"So?"

"People will talk."

"Let them."

"What if this doesn't work out? What about Alissa?"

"I'm in it for the long haul. If you and I don't work out, I think we're mature enough to stay civil to each other for our daughter's sake."

"Shhh," she urged, looking around to see if anyone was listening.

"I hope, at the very least, we can be friends."

"I'd like that," she said, tucking her hair behind her ear. "I'd like more."

Relief thudded through him. "Me too. Because you seem

to be a little embarrassed by me."

"It's weird being on a date with you. All the first-date awkwardness is missing, and yet…" She trailed off.

"It's still a little awkward."

"Yeah." She sighed in relief.

He let go of her hand while their lunch came. After the waiter left, Trent said, "Do you have any pictures of Alissa when she was a baby?"

"I have a whole album," she said. "She's my favorite subject. It's in New York, but I can ask my aunt to send it."

"I'd like to see it. I missed so much."

"I'm still pretty pissed at your manager," she said.

"Yeah, we had it out." Trent took a deep breath. "I found out you weren't the only one who contacted him about being pregnant."

She looked stricken and he immediately regretted his words.

"How many were there?" she asked.

"More than he thought was realistic. That's why he gave you such a hard time. He got an earful from me and he's investigating to see if anyone else was…" Trent's throat closed up and he had to take a long swallow of water "…pregnant with my child."

"So, Alissa could have half brothers and sisters," she said slowly.

"I wish I knew. If you had asked me a few days ago, I'd have said it was impossible. I always used protection."

Kelly nodded. "When the condom broke, I figured we were safe because I was on the pill. But I forgot to take it."

"I'm sorry I wasn't there for you. I would have made things right. You wouldn't have been alone."

"I probably wouldn't have been thrown out if I'd come clean to my dad."

It hurt to talk about this. He held her hands again. "We can't change the past. But we can make up for it. I'm not sure what kind of dad I can be. I'm still trying to figure out who I am without the rodeo. But I promise, you and Alissa will be taken care of."

She removed her hands from his. "We can take care of ourselves. Especially if it turns out you have other children."

"It doesn't seem likely that I have a bunch of kids I don't know about, but I'm going to make sure. I want to make things right."

"Good." Kelly fiddled with her napkin. "What if you find another one? Are you going to want to date their mother, too?"

"Date?" Trent shook his head. "No. I haven't stopped thinking about you since the night we were together. I don't even remember what the other women's names were. I know that sounds shitty. But it was one big party. I was young. I had more money than I knew what to do with. And nobody to tell me that just because I could do something, that didn't mean I should do it." He gave a half laugh. "I wonder sometimes what it would have been like if I rode Corazon del Diablo and hopped off like normal. Would I still be on tour, partying hard and drinking even harder? Or would it have gotten old by now?"

"You miss it," she said.

"I miss the exhilaration of the ride. I miss the excitement of testing my mettle against the bull. The rest of it doesn't seem so important."

"I wonder if I had tracked you down, would you have spent less time on the circuit? Would you have been on that bull, if you knew about Alissa?" Tears filled her eyes and she looked away.

"Aw, honey," he said, holding her hand again. "Yeah, I would have still been on the circuit. That was my job. And yeah, I would have asked for Corazon del Diablo because he was a tough son of a bitch and I wanted to prove I was tougher. What happened between me and the bull is not your fault and certainly not Alissa's."

She let out a shaky breath. "Thank you for that. It's been eating at me."

He kissed the back of her knuckles. "Let's put the past behind us. Let's start fresh today."

"What if you find out you have other kids?" she asked. "Where does that leave Alissa and me?"

"Will I want to be in my child's life? Yes. I grew up without a father and it was tough, so I don't want to do that to a child of mine. And do I want a friendly relationship with their mother? Absolutely. But you're the only one I want in my bed. There hasn't been anyone else since you."

She choked on her water. "In almost six years?"

"To be fair, a lot of the time I couldn't physically do anything without a lot of pain."

"What about now?"

He wasn't a 100% sure that now would be pain-free either, but he was willing to overlook that for her. "Was that an offer?"

She blushed. "Maybe."

He'd take maybe. It beat the hell out of no.

"There hasn't been anyone serious for me either. I went out on dates, but…" She shook her head. "No one serious."

"Good," he said. "We get to finish what we started."

"It's going to be a little tough with Alissa."

"It's going to be worth it."

"What happens if Alissa and I go back to New York?"

Trent forced himself not to react. He took a bite out of his sandwich and chewed slowly before answering. "If worse comes to worst, we can work out a visitation schedule."

She looked down at her plate. "I've never been without her for a day."

"I've never even had her for a day," he said, kindly.

"I know." Kelly blinked back tears.

"Hey," he said. "Nothing is certain. You may decide to stay in Last Stand or maybe I'll take my rodeo school up to New York."

Sputtering out a laugh, she said, "You'd move to New York?"

"If it meant being close to my daughter, I'd consider it."

"You'd be great in New York. If you could find a place that is. Leasing isn't as cheap up north as it is down here."

"I've got a long way to go until we get there. Let's concentrate on here and now. Finish your lunch and then we'll hit a matinee. This is a real date. I'll even spring for popcorn and licorice."

They caught up over lunch, talking about first-date things and seeing if they knew the same people from town. Then, they headed to the next town over for the movie theater. Trent bought tickets to see an action adventure flick he'd been itching to see. "Next time we can do the romantic comedy," he offered.

"I like action movies. The heroes are always hot."

"Oh yeah?" Trent slung his arm around her shoulder and she leaned her head against him. He was distracted by the warmth of her body and the sweet smell of her hair. He traced circles on her upper arm with his fingertips. She was so sweet to touch.

It occurred to him again that he really should bring up the paternity DNA test and the cheek swab sooner rather than later, but he didn't want to spoil this first date. He didn't need a test to know Alissa was his daughter. He felt it in his bones. Saw it in the way her eyes shone when she looked at him today. He wanted to believe Kelly was telling the truth and the test would take away any doubt and help them move forward.

After the movie, they walked out, hand in hand. He didn't want the day to end. He wanted more conversation, more kissing, and when they were through, more of his daughter.

As they pulled back onto the ranch, she let the car idle outside of the studio. He saw that someone had given Flower a trough of water and some hay. Trent would have to ask if there was a pasture she could roam around in when she wasn't working. But not right now. Right now, he brushed the hair away from Kelly's face.

"Thank you for going to lunch and a movie with me," he said, and leaned in for a kiss.

He couldn't resist a groan at the swipe of her tongue against his. Deepening the kiss, he slid his hand up her skirt. Her panties were damp and he pushed his fingers inside them. She came up off the seat and the car engine revved. Laughing, they broke apart and she turned the car off. "When's the futon coming?"

"This week," he said.

Reaching over to stroke him over his jeans, her eyes darkened with a need that almost had him dragging her out of the car to take her against the wall.

"I'd like to help you break it in."

"It's a date." He thumbed her hard nipple and circled it, over her thin blouse. "Unless you want to drive me back to the Bluebonnet Inn and we can indulge ourselves."

Her breathing was erratic and when she licked her lips, he went back in for another kiss. It took a moment before a buzzing sound broke them apart. Her phone.

"I've got to get this," she said shakily. "It's Janice, probably wondering where I am and what I'm doing. Alissa will be wondering too."

"I'll see you later." He couldn't resist one more kiss before getting out of the car.

Trent hoped that she would join him inside once she was done with her phone call, but he saw her drive off a few seconds later.

Soon, he promised himself. Soon, she'd be all his.

Chapter Nine

KELLY WORKED ALL night to get the backlog of work she'd been procrastinating on doing to Candace. She called her this morning to make sure everything was all right with her delivery.

"Hey, I'm sorry it took me so long. It's been a whirlwind."

"I understand. I normally wouldn't be so pushy, but the bride was hounding me. It looks great. Have you had a chance to open a bank account there yet?"

Groaning, Kelly added that to her list of things to do. "No. I'll get that done today and send you wiring instructions so you can pay me. Although I should have you send it directly to Home Depot."

"I think I have a line on someone looking for some rustic pictures for their engagement."

"We've got rustic. Where are they from?"

"They've got money to burn, so wherever they want to be. I'm going to check and see if they would be interested in a Texas ranch. The bride is a horse freak. How soon can you get me pictures of Pippi and Sunflower?"

"Today. Scour Janice's Facebook for pictures of Black

Dahlia and Synergy. They're heading back home. When are they looking to get these shots done?"

"As soon as possible."

Yes! This was just the break she needed.

"What other pictures can you get for me?" Candace asked. "You don't have an online portfolio set up yet, do you?"

Another item on the to-do list. "I can do a sunset shot this evening. End of this week, for the pavilion and the gazebo. Maybe."

"I'm going to quote them five grand—sound good?"

"Sounds good." Even with her aunt's commission, Kelly would have enough to reinvest in the business.

"Okay, I'll see what I can do."

After Kelly got off the phone with her aunt, she applied for a Home Depot credit card and got enough on it to buy the gazebo and a few other things. It wouldn't be perfect, but it would do for now. There were even a few bucks left over so she could buy the white paint.

Janice was out getting quotes for the retreat building and talking with a construction crew. Once her loan came in, they could get started. Janice was going to give notice to her job in Kentucky and then they were going to hope for the best and hit the ground running.

Early this morning, Janice had headed back to Kentucky with the horse trailer to pick up Synergy and Black Dahlia and the rest of her menagerie. Her father hadn't wanted her to go alone, so he'd had Nate go with her. Texas to Kentucky wasn't a bad trip, but Kentucky back to Texas with six dogs and two horses would probably try Nate's patience a bit. Sixteen hours there and sixteen hours back. Chances were, they'd miss the rodeo or at least be too tired to go.

While Nate was traveling with Janice, Kelly barely saw her father. He was gone before breakfast and she was usually out of the house by lunch. Dinner was a quiet affair. Her father was overdoing it and anything she said to suggest that maybe he was pushing himself was met with his temper.

"If I had sons instead of daughters, we wouldn't be in this mess," he had snarled at her.

Kelly almost asked him what he was doing out there that required a penis, but Alissa was at the table, making herself as small as possible, so Kelly let it go. Although it killed her not to say anything at all. That wasn't the lesson she wanted to teach her daughter.

And yet when they were all younger, they'd gone out on the cattle drives. Her father had insisted on it. Emily loved to round up the strays and herd them back where they belonged. Janice was interested in the cattle themselves, and could spot a sick one quickly so they could be isolated from the herd and given treatment, if necessary. And while they were doing that, Kelly and her father were riding fences and repairing them as needed. She had loved that time when it had been just the two of them. He would tell stories about his rodeo days and they would talk about the bull riders and the bulls they thought were going to be famous. They had talked about Trent. Her father said he admired the kid and knew that he was going to be a star. Kelly wondered what would be the best way to tell him that the bull rider was

Alissa's father.

"If you want, Emily and I can go out tomorrow." It would give her an opportunity to build her portfolio and maybe get some pictures to sell to Getty or another stock photo place.

"No," he said, shaking his head. "You're both too green."

He wasn't wrong, but at least they were a lot younger and healthier than he was. Kelly knew better than to say that, though.

"Can't you do something?" she asked her mother.

Sarah just shook her head. "You know how he gets. He should have gone with Janice and left Nate."

Thirty-two hours in the car with her father? Kelly figured Janice would drive off a cliff if she was trapped with him that long. So while he and the rest of the ranch hands rotated the cows to the next pasture, she took the liberty of using his truck to go pick up her gazebo.

"You want to come with me?" she asked Alissa.

They had spent time yesterday doing a puzzle and while she enjoyed playing with her daughter, her mind drifted to Trent, wondering what he was doing.

"No. MeMaw and I are going to pick the last of the blueberries for pancakes to celebrate Aunt Emily coming home."

"She won't be here until next week," Kelly said.

"We'll freeze them, because they're not going to last," Sarah said, hugging her granddaughter to her. "I'm so happy Alissa's here. She brightens my day. Spending time with her is a nice relief from going over the books and accounting."

"I'm glad, Mom."

There was more she wanted to say to her mother, but she didn't know where to begin. Kelly wasn't sure she was happy to be here. She was still waiting for the other shoe to drop. Maybe if she trusted her mother more, she could tell her who Alissa's father was and her mom could suggest a way to break it gently to her father. But her mind kept going back to the night she left, when all her mother did was cry as Kelly drove off the ranch.

On impulse, she stopped by Trent's studio and was happy to see him there, stocking shelves with newly branded equipment. She saw that he'd set up a few training machines and she went over to one.

"Can I try it out?" Kelly grinned.

"Grab a glove." Trent pointed to the pile of them. "I'll set it up for you." He wrapped a rope harness around it. "You ever done this before?" Pulling out a few mats, he placed them all around.

"Does riding a barrel at my cousin's Fourth of July party count?"

"Close enough."

He helped her climb on top of it and kept his hands on her waist. She liked his hands there. "It's tippy. You got a good seat?"

"Um, you tell me."

"I think that's a trick question, ma'am," he drawled. "Grab the rope with your gloved hand."

She did.

"Other hand up."

Kelly put her hand in the air.

"You ready?"

"I'm ready."

He let go of her and moved around to the back. Picking up the large lever, he pumped it slow and turned around. "Not bad. Nice technique. Let's try a spin." Still pushing the lever to make the seat go up and down, he walked in a circle. She bent and tried to hold on, but wound up sliding off and landing on her butt on the mat.

"Dismount needs work, but looking good on my end." He held out a hand to help her up.

Part of her wanted to tug him down with her. But her things-to-do list wasn't getting any smaller. When she got to her feet, though, she put her arms around his neck and kissed him because she could.

It was pure pleasure to be in his arms. There was no rush. No urgency, just the sexy slide of his mouth and his hard body rubbing against her.

"You want to go for a ride to Home Depot with me?" she asked when they came up for air.

"And people think the magic is gone in some relation-ships." Trent smiled and it did crazy things to her already rampaging libido.

"You got that futon yet?" She might like to be talked into delaying her shopping trip for a chance to spend some alone time with him.

"Not yet," he drawled. "Let me lock up here and I'll take a ride with you. Is Alissa coming with us?"

"No, she and MeMaw have plans."

His smiled dimmed. "I would have liked to have spent some time together, just the three of us."

"It's hard with all the work I have planned and you getting your school together." She laid her head on his chest. "Soon. I promise. Maybe you can have dinner with us later?"

"I'd like that."

"It won't be just the three of us, but Janice won't be there. My parents will, but my father will pretty much be a zombie. If he doesn't fall asleep in his mashed potatoes, he'll be snoring on the couch. He's been working full days with the cattle and I think if his doctor found out, he'd be in big trouble."

"Does your dad know you have his truck?"

"No, why?"

"I was wondering if it would get back to him that it was parked in front of the Bluebonnet Inn."

She grinned at him. "I said we were going to Home Depot, not back to your hotel room."

He shrugged. "Can't blame a guy for trying."

"I'm not sure if he'd be more pissed that it was outside your hotel room or that I went to Home Depot without him."

She helped Trent put the exercise mats back next to the stability balls and returned the glove while he coiled the rope back up.

"When I was a kid, the Home Depot was a big deal," Kelly said. "We used to go in there to get stuff that we needed to fix things on the ranch. I was in charge of the tape measure."

"That's an important job," Trent said, locking up.

"Measure twice, cut once. Although with my dad, it was more, measure four times and curse when it still wasn't right. It didn't stop him from doing it all over again the next weekend. Was your dad a weekend warrior?"

"Never met the man. I don't even know his name."

Kelly winced. "Sorry, I forgot."

Trent shrugged and got into the truck. "Mama said he was a bullfighter, but that was about it."

"Does your mom still live around here?"

"She died when I was in high school."

"Oh man, I'm batting a thousand on the questions today."

"It doesn't bother me much anymore."

"Still, I can't imagine losing my mom. She and I have had our ups and downs. It was hard to forgive her for not taking my side against my father, but in the end, I went to New York and she had to live with him afterward. So, I eventually understood." Things were never the same though.

"My mom was never interested in being a mom. She was a buckle bunny and during the rodeo season, I had to fend for myself or at least make myself scarce. Luckily, my best friend Pete had a big family, so they barely noticed one more kid."

"I'm glad you had somewhere to go."

"After she drank herself to death, Billy became my official guardian. We stayed at the Bluebonnet Inn for two years while I finished school and then we traveled the world. I was in Brazil for my twenty-first birthday."

"Do you miss traveling?"

"Yeah, but I wish I'd explored the places I went to a little more. Most of the time, I only saw the inside of the arena and the inside of my hotel room. I'd like to go back and look around a bit, experience the culture."

"I haven't been out of the U.S. One day, I'd like to take a cruise to some exotic island. Maybe when Alissa is older."

"Does she swim?"

"She knows how to. I took her for lessons at the YMCA."

"Can she fish?"

"Not yet. My dad will probably buy her first pole this Christmas."

"Not if I beat him to it."

Kelly groaned. "You do not want to get into a pissing match with my father."

"He's going to have to play nice, or I'm not going to invite him along on the daddy daughter fishing trip."

"Is that right? Am I invited?"

Trent stroked his cheek while he saucily pretended to think about the question. "Depends. Do you bait your own hook?"

"Of course, I do. Because *my* daddy taught me."

"You can come, then."

"You've got this daddy thing all planned out," she said lightly. She should be happy about this. So why did it feel so threatening?

"I'm beginning to see what I've missed out on. Pete is married with two kids. He has a job he likes and he takes care of his mom, the way she used to take care of us. Billy and I have lived out of motel rooms most of our lives. It's going to be hard to get used to having my own place. When does the maid clean up the room?"

"When you tell her to." Kelly grinned. "Or you can make your own damned bed."

She parked the truck and they went into the store.

"Do you have your tape measure?" he asked.

Tapping her forehead, she grabbed a large flatbed cart. "I have it all up here."

"I'm glad one of us does."

She wheeled the cart toward the patio section of the store, refusing to be distracted by any of the sales or interesting items on the endcaps.

"What are we here for again?" he asked, checking out a power washer.

"Gazebo. And some white paint and a paint sprayer and brushes. Depends on the prices, though."

"Trent, is that you?"

Kelly had just maneuvered the cart down the aisle, but the feminine drawl made her glance back and do a double take. Closing in on Trent was a bodacious ex-cheerleader with big hair squeezed into a tiny dress. She had a Gucci purse slung over her arm and her nails could be lethal weapons.

"Hi," he said, stepping back as she gave him a big hug. He twisted his face to the side so when she tried to kiss him on the mouth, she got his cheek.

"It's me, Darlene."

"Yeah, I remember." He shot a panicked look at Kelly,

but she just raised an eyebrow and crossed her arms over her chest.

"We live a few towns over, but our store was out of stock on the gas grill we wanted. I can't believe you're here." She squeezed the muscles on his arms and Kelly abandoned the cart and started walking over. "We can't wait for the rodeo on Saturday." Darlene gestured and a boy about seven or eight came up to him. "This is my son, Kevin. Kevin this is one of Mommy's friends."

Kelly saw Trent freeze up and do mental math and come up stricken. Did he think Kevin was his son? He really didn't know. Had there been that many women? It made her feel like she'd just been one of the crowd. Still, Kelly guessed she'd known that and it hadn't mattered at the time. Maybe if they had tried to make it work, it would have come between them. She looked the boy over and didn't see a resemblance, but that didn't mean anything. How many kids could be Trent's? How many half siblings did Alissa have? There was a sharp pain in her chest and she rubbed it, hoping it was heartburn and not heartbreak. Again.

"Do you like rodeo?" Trent asked the boy, recovering quickly.

Kevin nodded. "I want to be a bull rider, like my daddy."

Trent choked and coughed. "Who's that?"

Darlene laughed and patted Trent's cheek. "My husband, John Miller."

Kelly saw the moment when Trent realized he was off the hook. His smile became more natural and the stiffness left his body. "I hope to see him on Saturday."

JAMIE K. SCHMIDT

"He'll be there. We'll all be there, Trent. I'm glad you're okay."

Kelly slung her arm around Trent's waist. "He's opening up a bull-riding school at the Three Sisters Ranch."

"You are?" Darlene said, eyes wide. "For adults or kids?"

"Kids, at the moment."

"Can I go, Mom?" Kevin said.

"Sure. I mean I've got to discuss it with your daddy, but I don't see why not."

"I've got to get some business cards made up," Trent said. "But there will be plenty of information at the rodeo this weekend."

"I can't wait."

Darlene didn't try for another kiss while Kelly was standing there, but she did put a little sway in her step when she walked away. Who wore heels to walk around a warehouse?

"John Miller's a good rider," Trent said, sounding dazed.

"I haven't been watching lately." Kelly steered him back toward the patio aisle.

"Thanks for helping me out there. My head is not right. For a moment, I thought…"

"Yeah, you thought Kevin was yours. Did you sleep with Darlene?"

He shrugged. "Maybe. Probably. She seems like my type."

Kelly pulled away from him, stung. If Darlene was his type, what did that make her? Kelly was a sturdy farm girl, who only teased her hair out for the rodeo. "You really don't remember?"

148

"Most nights, I was either drunk or on my way to getting that way. There were a lot of women at the parties and all of them were eager to go home with the bull riders and bull-fighters. We had fun. We never thought of the consequences."

"Are you sure you don't miss that?"

"Not as much as I thought I would. But I do miss the rodeo. I'm looking forward to this weekend. It'll be hard not lining up for a bull. It's tempting to just do one last ride."

"What would happen if you did?"

Trent grimaced. "A world of pain. Setbacks. Humiliation. Billy would kill me. I wouldn't be able to ride a horse for a while, if ever. Depends on how bad I land."

"It's not worth it," she said, laying a hand on his arm until he looked at her.

"I know," he said. "Well, my head knows. And I'm pretty sure my leg and hip are aware of the consequences, but every now and then, I think I've got one more ride in me. No one likes going out a loser."

"You're not a loser."

"I didn't mean it like that. I meant it like, the bull won and it wasn't my choice not to try again."

"A concussion and a few broken bones will do that for you."

"You know what they say. Blood washes off. Bruises go away. Bones heal. Scars show character. Pain is temporary, but victory? That's forever. I saw that on a T-shirt once." He grinned at her. "It's like poetry in the rhythm, so I remember it."

"Does that really work? Memorizing poetry to help with your physical therapy?"

"It did for me. But I think it's the message that sticks with you and the cadence of it that helps you take your mind off things. You should try it."

"I will, the next time a bull knocks me off." She smiled at him and moved down the aisle, staring at the bins to find the boxes she wanted. It was a do-it-yourselfer and she was hoping that she could get some of the ranch hands to help her build it. Otherwise, it was probably going to be lopsided.

"It works for mental therapy too. If you're feeling anxious or worried. Memorizing a poem gives your brain something to focus on other than your problems."

"All the poems I know are nursery rhymes."

"There are lessons in them too. What type of poems does Alissa like to listen to?"

"She likes Dr. Seuss and Shel Silverstein."

"Maybe, I could come over and read some to her?"

Kelly nodded. "Sure, that would be great."

"Tonight, after dinner?"

She took a deep breath. "I think that would be all right. Have you memorized any children's poems?"

"Not that I can remember, off the top of my head. Mostly it's just lines that come back to me. Odd phrases that flit around in my head."

"Who's your favorite poet?"

"I really don't have one. It was whoever my physical therapist put on during our workout sessions."

"You ever woo a woman with poetry?" She found the

boxes she needed. "Here, help me with these. I need these five."

"No, but there were a few lines I stashed away because I thought they might get me laid someday." He hauled one of the boxes onto the cart.

"Hit me with one. Are you sure you're okay with lifting these?"

"Yeah, as long as you don't want me to carry them around the store. Taking them off the shelf and putting them on the cart is fine."

"I'm waiting," she said, as they moved on down the aisle.

Trent took her in his arms. It happened so whirlwind fast that she clung to him for balance. "I burn, then freeze. Enslaved by foul caprice. And only Kelly's arms can grant me peace."

She blinked up at him. "Are you shitting me?"

"It's iambic pentameter. Chicks dig that."

Kelly cocked her head at him. "Are you for real?"

"Shut up and kiss me," he whispered and covered her mouth with his.

Chapter Ten

I T FELT GOOD to be back in his rodeo clothes and back in the saddle. Trent let the exhilaration of the crowd pour over him as he rode into the ring to announce the VIPs and special guests. He looked for Kelly in the stands, but only caught glimpses of her strawberry-blonde ponytail as she took pictures. Billy was handing out flyers about the rodeo school and taking down names on his clipboard.

He hadn't had any more time with Alissa or Kelly after that one dinner the other night. He did get to read his baby girl all the Dr. Seuss books she wanted until she fell asleep, just like her mother had. He had tucked both his girls in, giving their foreheads a kiss and then went back to his place to work.

The organizers of the rodeo had him bustling to and from events. At his autograph signing, he was both proud and humbled by the line of people waiting for him. He posed for pictures and grinned until his face hurt. It went on for so long that his meet and greet with the press had to be cut short. As he was being led away to the next event, a reporter jockeyed in front of them.

"Trent," she said, handing him her business card. "I'm

Lana Kirkland. I was hoping to stop by your school next week for an interview."

"Sounds great. Call my manager, Billy King, to set things up." He shook her hand and when their eyes met, he felt a spark of recognition. But it was gone when his handlers jostled him away.

"Been there. Done that." He heard her say.

He whirled back to find her, but she was lost in the crowd. His heartbeat was loud in his ears, drowning out the crowd. Was she another woman Billy had railroaded? So far, the private investigator Billy had hired to look in on the women who took Billy's money hadn't found anything that pointed to Trent being a father. One woman did have a child the right age, but she had been logged into a DNA site that searched for ancestors and family members. The detective had been able to compare Trent's sample with the child's and they weren't a match.

Trent had been fascinated by the results and sent in a cheek swab to see if they could find some long-lost relative of his. If they could connect a serial killer to victims in a decades-old case, maybe this company could find out who his father was. Maybe it would connect Trent with a son or daughter. He didn't tell Billy he was doing this, because his manager would probably pitch a fit about opening himself up to lawsuits, but that was the last thing Trent was worried about.

Next up was the rodeo court announcement, so that meant he had to get back on the horse. He made sure to tape up his knee for support and take a bunch of Advil so no one caught him wincing on the way up or down.

Everything was going just fine until he dismounted to judge the mutton busting, and he caught sight of the waiting pens where the bulls were. Frank Sullivan was chatting with Enrique Chavez, one of the top breeders of champion bulls. But that barely registered because behind Chavez was his nemesis—Corazon del Diablo.

The bull looked at him and Trent felt a frisson of awareness. That son of a bitch was pure evil. Mexican fighting bulls were bred for aggression and it showed. Trent bared his teeth at it. It stared back at him with flat eyes with a hint of crazy in them. The world narrowed to the two of them. Six seconds on that bull's back had changed his life forever.

Six seconds. Two more seconds and it could have ended differently. Two more seconds and he would have gone out a champion. Two more seconds and Trent could have placated himself that at least he went out on top of his game, instead of underneath this bull's hooves.

Before he could approach the bull and his owner, Chavez, a few of Trent's old buddies smacked him on the back and dragged him away to hang out with the younger riders. Corazon del Diablo hadn't been on the lists of bulls for the event. He would have remembered that. He must have been a late admission.

"I can't stay long," he said to the bull riders, because he could see the kids lining up for their sheep run. He couldn't see Alissa, but he hoped she'd be there with her pink leather-fringed chaps and matching gear. "Who's slotted to ride Corazon del Diablo?"

"I am." A young, brash kid strutted forth and gave him a cocky grin. "I'm Johnny Trapp. It's nice to meet you, Trent. I saw the footage that took you out. Don't worry, I'm going to last eight seconds and put an end to that bull's rep."

Of course you are, kid. It was what Trent would have said to the old-timer when he was Trapp's age. He knew better than to warn him off the bull. That would just piss Trapp off. But he felt he had to tell him something, just in case Trapp ended up in the same situation he'd been in.

"Well, here's what you need to do." Trent remembered every instant of his ride. He had played it over and over in his head. "He's going to come out of the chute fighting. Expect him to buck high and spin like a tornado in midair. He whips around fast and he'll try and slam his head back to get you with his horns. Once you're down, he's going to go for you. Be prepared. Roll up right away, fast as you can. He has to be forced back into the pen."

"I got this. He's slower now than when you had him. He's getting old. Talk is Chavez is putting him out to pasture after this. You sure you don't want another try at him?"

Did he? Trent's entire body locked up. Hell yeah, every inch of him screamed. But it wasn't his night to shine. He'd had his time. It was over. He was a teacher now and there wasn't anything wrong with that. He was also a father. He couldn't afford to be reckless when his daughter needed him. Except she didn't know he was her father. Wouldn't it be better if she remembered him as a winner and not some limping old man who taught her how to ride a sheep? It was hard to turn away, but Trent did.

"He's your ride, kid. Just be safe."

But it bothered the fuck out of him. So much that he couldn't enjoy the mutton-busting event and nearly missed Alissa's ride. She made it to the second round, but fell off right out of the chute on her second ride. She got up like a trooper, though, and he resisted the urge to go over and check to make sure she was okay. He did get a hug when he awarded her with her participation ribbon and medal. And if he held on to her a little longer than the other kids who hugged him, well, he was sure no one noticed.

Kelly got some great shots of the entire event and he hoped she was taking pictures when he gave Alissa her prize. He definitely wanted a copy of that for himself.

After doing more announcing work, he was back down with the bull riders. The bullfighters were top notch and he high-fived one of the guys who had helped him out on more than one occasion. Last Stand had a rule that the riders had to wear helmets and chest pads. The riders groaned about it, though. Let 'em bitch. The second one of them landed on their head and cracked the helmet instead of their skull, they would shut up about it.

Trent was tense and jittery as hell as they brought Corazon del Diablo into the chute.

"You want to hot prod him, Trent?" the gate man asked.

Shaking his head, Trent laughed without humor. "You won't need to."

As if to prove his point, the bull stomped and slammed against the pen, bucking up and nearly throwing Johnny off in the chute. The flank man tried to steady the bull. The chute boss was there helping him keep his seat and the rope puller was handing him his rope. Trent didn't let himself think too much about it, but he hopped over the fence and stood next to the gate man. There was a three-man bullfighter team and a horseman with a rope. They kept the crowd motivated and cheering while Johnny got settled on the bull's back.

When Johnny gave the nod, the gate man slammed open the gate. Corazon del Diablo went airborne. A bull that big shouldn't be able to jump that high. He kicked and turned ninety degrees. He touched the ground for a moment and spun fast. Johnny had a good seat and kept it throughout all the twists, turns, and shuffles the bull threw at him. Johnny made it eight seconds.

"Yes!" Trent clapped his hands.

But then the bull tossed him and Trent saw that Johnny's spur was caught in his rope. Hung up, Johnny hit the ground hard on his shoulder. The bull twisted and stomped down. The bullfighters were there pushing and distracting the bull, but Johnny was being dragged across the arena, dangerously close to Corazon del Diablo's hooves. The horseman whipped his lasso and missed. Damn it. Trent grabbed a red T-shirt and waded in, waving it furiously.

"Hey! Hey!" Trent cursed at it in gutter Spanish that he'd picked up on the circuit and from what Pete had taught him.

Corazon del Diablo caught sight of him and tossed his head. One of the bullfighters took a hold of the rope hook and the other used a knife to cut the rope free just as the bull charged Trent. The gate to the pen opened. The lasso hooked Corazon del Diablo by his filed-down horns. Trent leapt for the rails and got up in time to miss the charge and with a little more encouragement, the bull went back into the pens, snorting and kicking all the way.

Johnny hadn't moved. The paramedics were out and after a few moments helped him to his feet. He waved to the crowd and they roared in relief. He limped off and Trent followed them back.

After a few minutes of examination, the doctor came out and gave a short summary to the chute boss. "Fractured his ankle," the doctor said. "Dislocated shoulder and a concussion."

Trent sighed in relief. The kid would ride again.

"I'm all right," Johnny said. "What did I score?"

"Eighty-six."

"All right." He accepted some high fives. Trent left the area just as his knees began to wobble. That could have been his last ride. He could have gone eight seconds and gotten away with a concussion. But the adrenaline that now coursed through him, that was what he'd really missed.

"Are you out of your mind?" Kelly rammed into him, furious. The force of it almost took them both to the ground. Luckily, they hit the side of the building and he was able to keep his feet.

"I was fine," he said, anger pouring out of him now that reaction had set in.

"You could have been hurt."

He shrugged her off him. "It's all good." He wanted his shot on that bull. He wanted to ride it more than eight seconds. He wanted to be on its back until it stopped bucking and stood still like a sheep. It would never happen. And his hip would probably shatter on a hard bounce. That pissed him off and he banged his fist on the side of the building.

Kelly flinched away from him. "What were you thinking?"

"That I wasn't going to let that devil bull end another cowboy's career."

"So, you jumped in the ring? Let the bullfighters do their job."

"I did. The more hands the better. Johnny's safe, and now I've got to go back to the booth to make some announcements."

He stormed away from her before realizing what he was doing. Then, pivoting, he came back to where she was standing, still gaping at him. Hauling her to him, he kissed her hard, not caring who saw them.

Her fingers tangled in his hair as she stood up on her tiptoes to meet his mouth with a forceful kiss of her own.

"Trent," she groaned.

Anger turned to passion and against sane reasoning, he backed her toward the equipment room. Still kissing her, he fumbled the door open and kicked it shut behind them. It was his lucky day—she was wearing a long prairie skirt. Kelly unbuckled his pants, her mouth and tongue never leaving his. Pulling up her skirt to her waist, he took out his buck knife and cut her panties off her. She moaned as the little scraps of silk fluttered to the equipment floor along with the knife. Trent's fingers found her wet and eager for him. He fingered her quickly, enjoying her reactions as she gasped and writhed. Clearing a shelf with his forearm, he lifted her up on it and draped her legs over his shoulders.

He dove his head under her skirt, tonguing her pussy. Kelly grabbed his head, crying out in pleasure. Her musky sweet taste was pushing him over the limit and he licked her clit and sucked on the folds of her skin when her thighs trembled.

"Trent," she begged.

It had been over five years since he'd had her like this. Damn, it was just as good as he remembered. He flicked his tongue over that throbbing bud until she writhed on his face. She was on fire for him, egging him on with each excited gasp.

There were no words, just moans and the building need that he had to have her right then. Right now. She held him against her sweetness while she came.

"Damn," he panted. "I need you."

"Yes," she gritted out, nearly vibrating with anticipation.

Trent pulled a condom out of his pants and ripped it open. He licked her slowly as he undid his pants and pulled them down. Her thighs quivered against his cheeks. After he slid on the condom, he came up for air. Kelly was panting, her eyes half closed. Picking her up from the shelf, he turned and pressed her back against the wall. She wrapped her legs around him as he eased inside her.

Kelly's back arched and she cried out again, clutching his shoulders.

"All right?" he grunted out, burying his face in her neck.

"Fuck me," she moaned.

Grinning, he let loose, thrusting his hips hard into her hot, willing pussy. Pain and discomfort from his abused body merged into a burning pleasure as he pumped inside her. Trent sucked on her neck, as she tangled her fingers through his hair. The greedy sounds of pleasure she was making sent him closer and closer to the edge. It was the night they met, all over again. He took her faster, slamming into her as she begged him for more. She tightened around him and she came shouting, "Yes, Trent. Yes."

As she clamped around him, he started to lose focus and began to shake. His orgasm ripped through him with the force of a Texas twister and he groaned in quick guttural grunts.

"Later," he promised her, kissing her lips as he eased out of her. "Later, we'll do this slow. Come to the studio and spend the night."

"I can't," she said, her legs shaking when he eased them to the ground.

"Yes, you can." Trent smoothed her skirt down. "After everyone is asleep. Take Pippi and ride out. When you come back in the morning, everyone will think you were out for a sunrise ride. Please, Kelly. I'm not done with you and I've got to get back before they miss me. Please, say you'll come."

"I'll come," she said, softly.

"Yes, you will." He tossed the condom in the trash and

put himself back together, picking up his knife from the floor. "You're so beautiful." He kissed her once again because he couldn't stop himself, but then forced himself to pull away. "I'll be waiting for you."

"I'll be there." Kelly touched her lips. They were puffy from his kisses. He almost went back for more when they heard voices outside the door.

"Come on," Trent said, hooking an arm around her and pulling her forward. "Here, take these." He handed her a box of prizes for the kids while he grabbed a case of soda. When they left the supply shed, no one gave them a second glance.

"Where do these go?" she asked.

"Damned if I know. Let's set them by the stage."

"Trent, you stay away from that bull," she said, once they'd put their packages down on a table. "I mean it." She tugged at his sleeve.

"All I'm thinking about is you," he said. "You better be getting back before Alissa wonders where you are. I want to do something as a family tomorrow."

"Okay." She nodded. "I have some things to do in the morning, but we can come over later."

He gave her a quick hug. "I can't wait until tonight when we can take our time."

She gave his ass a quick squeeze. "I kind of like the fast and furious."

"I can do that, too."

He swatted her butt as she left. He was glad she'd taken his mind off Corazon del Diablo before he'd done something stupid, like borrow some rope and climb on top of the bastard.

Chapter Eleven

KELLY TUCKED ALISSA into bed. She had cried when Kelly told her Trent couldn't tuck her in again tonight because he would be up late with the rodeo. Sticky with cotton candy and filled up with popcorn, Alissa accepted a cowboy bear instead. She named it Trent and it was currently wearing her mutton-busting medal. Alissa had nearly fallen asleep in her bath, and Kelly was ready to join her. But she took a bracing hot shower instead, putting on her favorite perfume and a matching set of bra and panties. If Trent wanted to cut these off her, he was damned sure going to pay for the replacements.

She downloaded the pictures she'd taken and sorted them into categories to touch up later. Kelly had also handed out some business cards and made a few contacts. Luckily, she didn't need a studio. These parents wanted action shots of their kids on the go and she could edit the pictures from right here.

As she waited for the house to settle down, she shared the video she'd taken of Alissa riding the sheep with her sisters. Emily was in the airport now and would soon be on her way home. She was excited that they'd soon be all together and be able to affect the ranch's bottom line.

It was closer to one in the morning when she made her way out to the stable with an overnight bag. The lights were on inside and she could hear a lot of commotion. She walked in hesitantly and was surprised to see Janice and Nate guiding Synergy into a stall. The high-strung stallion was balking and misbehaving, but the two of them weren't taking any of his nonsense.

"You're back early," she said, tossing the bag down so she could help.

Janice hugged her after they secured the racehorse inside. "We pushed through to try and get to the rodeo, but the traffic did us in. We saw the fireworks from the highway."

"Hi, Nate," Kelly said, hugging him as well.

He was a big bear of a man with kind tawny eyes and short brown hair. She didn't think she'd ever seen him without a cowboy hat on. "How's your dad?" he asked.

"Tired, ornery. I bet he'll be thrilled you're back. He's been overdoing it. But if you want, hide your truck and I'll tell him I never saw you so you can sleep in tomorrow."

"Tempting," he said.

Kelly followed them back to the trailer while they took Black Dahlia out.

"Come on, ugly," Nate said, guiding the gorgeous mare out.

"Don't come crying to me if she bites you," Janice said, going into the extended cab for the dog cages. Kelly helped her take the six cages out and put them on the barn floor. Once Black Dahlia was settled in, Nate said, "I'm going to bed."

He leaned in and kissed Janice on the mouth and then walked away, as if he hadn't just dropped a bomb in the stable.

"What the hell?" Kelly whispered, frantically clicking leashes on the dogs before they could escape their cages and take off.

Janice blushed. "I'm not sure what's gotten into him." She took three dogs and Kelly took the other three. As they walked the excited pups of all shapes and sizes, Janice asked, "What are you doing out so late?"

"I'm sneaking out to join Trent. He's staying at the school."

"Pretty ballsy," she said. "You better hope Alissa doesn't wake up in the middle of the night."

"After the day she's had, I don't think she'll be up before dawn. But just in case, were you planning on joining Nate in his room off the bunkhouse?"

"No," Janice said, her voice cracking into the night air in a horrified screech.

"Shh," Kelly admonished her.

"It's not like that between us," Janice whispered fiercely.

"That was a pretty good kiss, by the looks of things."

"It's nothing. Just nothing. Drop it, okay."

"One condition."

Janice narrowed her eyes. "What?"

"Sleep in my bed, in case Alissa gets up. And cover for me in the morning, if I'm not back in time."

"That's two conditions," Janice said primly.

"Or I could ask Nate what was up with that kiss."

"Don't you dare."

Kelly shrugged and waited.

"Fine," Janice sighed. "What do you want me to say if anyone asks where you are?"

"Tell them I went for a morning ride."

"Uh-huh, I bet you'll be riding all right."

"Janice." Kelly rolled her eyes.

"Help me get the dogs in the house and I'll do it."

"You want them back in the cages?"

"No, the poor things have been cooped up enough. They'll sleep in bed with me and probably with Alissa. She likes dogs, right?"

"She loves them. Thanks."

As the dogs finished up their business and Janice cleaned up after them, she asked, "Are you sure you know what you're doing? I wouldn't want to see you get hurt."

"I'm sure about Trent. I've loved him forever. And now it seems like we're going to finally get our chance to be together."

"I hope so, Kelly. Does Alissa like him?"

"Yes. He's made a big impression on her."

"Is he going to stick around here?" Janice asked pointedly.

"I guess that depends on the school, but I think he's in it for the long haul." Kelly really wanted to tell her sister the whole truth, about Trent being Alissa's father, but it was too late for what would no doubt be a long conversation and she wanted to tell both her sisters at the same time.

They brought the dogs in the house as quietly as they could. She could hear her father snoring, so they made it up to her room without incident. The dogs were relieved to be out of the truck and off their leashes. After investigating several smells and no marking of territory, they settled around the room.

"You're going to trip on the way to the bathroom," Kelly said, trying to maneuver her way back to the door without stepping on someone's tail.

"Nah, watch." Janice got into bed and all six dogs joined her.

"Mom's going to shit if she sees that."

"Have fun, and close the door behind you."

Shaking her head, Kelly crept back downstairs and back to the barn. She set up the dog kennels in a neat line and took out Pippi, who was more interested in her new neighbors than going for a ride, but she allowed Kelly to saddle her and ride out.

It was a beautiful, clear night. The full moon lit up everything, so Kelly didn't even need her flashlight. She couldn't help but feel the excitement build, and she kicked Pippi into a controlled gallop. There was a light on in the studio and in the barn, and her heart fluttered.

Heading toward the barn, she met Trent coming out.

"I was hoping you hadn't changed your mind."

"Never," she said. "Are you sure you're not too tired?"

"Not for you." He helped her dismount and she led Pippi to the barn. He had set up a stall for her. "You're not wandering around tonight," he said to the horse. "You can keep Flower company."

Kelly took off the saddle and made sure Pippi was comfortable and had everything she needed. Trent leaned up against the barn door, watching her, and she realized she was stalling.

"Ready?" he asked in a husky tone.

"More than ready." She took his hand as he shut off the lights and secured the barn door. They strolled back to the studio.

"How did the rest of the night go?" he asked.

"We had to get Alissa to bed before she melted down into a tired little rodeo princess puddle. How about for you?"

"Great. Everybody was headed over to the Last Stand Saloon, but I couldn't wait to get back home to you."

Home.

Kelly smiled. "It was hard sneaking out. Janice and Nate caught me."

"Is that going to cause trouble?" They went inside the studio.

"No, Janice will keep her mouth shut and Nate's not going to open up this bag of worms."

"Last time I checked, you were over twenty-one."

"Not to my dad."

"Are we going to tell him soon?"

She sighed. "I'm afraid to."

Trent frowned. "Afraid of him physically?"

"No." She shook her head. "It's stupid, but I'm afraid he's going to throw me out again. I mean intellectually, I know I can go back to New York with my aunt or hell, rent an apartment anywhere I like. But it's like I'm trapped in time. I'm still that waddling, blubbery mess going to my car and looking back at them on the porch—my father purple-faced and shouting and my mother silently crying." Kelly took in a deep shuddering breath. "I don't want Alissa to ever see that side of her memaw and pawpaw. It took me a long time to forgive them."

"Did you? Because I sure don't."

"Trent, you don't know what it was like."

"I know they threw the mother of my child out when she needed them the most. I know they ignored my daughter's existence for the first few years of her life."

"My mother didn't."

"I don't care. She let you go."

"She knew I was going to her sister. She knew I'd be safe."

"It's not good enough, Kelly."

And it wasn't. Kelly wasn't even sure why she was defending her parents, except she didn't like hearing Trent condemn them.

"I should have…"

He held her shoulders and looked down into her eyes. She was mesmerized by the intense blue of his gaze. "They should have. Or rather, they shouldn't have kicked you out of your home."

She sniffed. "It was probably time for me to move out anyway."

Trent kissed her forehead. "I get it. They're your parents and Alissa's grandparents. But I'm still pissed at them."

"Thanks." She hugged him.

"And you don't ever have to worry about your father's reactions again. You come to me if things get crazy. We'll figure something out. I can wait a little longer."

After locking the door, Trent led her upstairs. Her heart was fluttering in her chest and she realized that telling everyone he was Alissa's father wasn't the catastrophe she'd been building up in her head.

"As soon as Emily gets here next week, I'm going to tell them that you're Alissa's father. Then, my dad."

"I like that. Progress. When are we telling Alissa?"

"Soon. My dad first, then Alissa."

The loft was set up like a bachelor's bedroom. It was stark, but functional.

"Are you really going to live here?" she asked.

"Why not? Bathroom and showers are downstairs. I've got a kitchenette off the office." He sat on his futon and pulled off his boots. "There's the TV. The only thing missing is you." Trent patted the place next to him on the futon.

Kelly sat down, nerves coming back again.

"Now then," he said, taking her boots off. "Where were we?"

Unbuttoning his shirt one pearl button at a time, she pressed tiny kisses over his forehead, eyelids, and face. Trent shrugged out of the shirt. His T-shirt was next. She pulled it up over his arms and tossed it aside. Kelly slid her hand over the rough texture of his chest and down lower.

"My turn," he said huskily and pulled her shirt over her

head. After unsnapping her bra, he flung it on the floor and groaned in appreciation at her breasts. Trent pulled her back onto the futon with him. She was flat on her back while he lay on his side, resting his head on his hand. He traced the curves of her breasts, circling one nipple until it puckered tightly. He did the same to the other one before dipping his head to suck on the sensitive peaks.

Kelly gasped, threading her fingers through his silky hair as he indulged himself with long pulls, using his tongue and the slightest bit of teeth. Her jeans were too tight and he was wearing too many pieces of clothing.

"God, I've been thinking about having you like this for years," he whispered.

He kissed her, his mouth hot and wet on hers. Her fingers trembled as she unfastened his Levi's and pushed them down his narrow hips. Kicking them and his underwear off, he was gloriously naked and she eagerly touched every inch of him within reach as they kissed.

Taking off her jeans and panties, he knelt between her thighs and reached over to the small table next to the bed. When he pulled out a box of condoms, she said, "Not yet." Pulling him down, she pushed him so he was on his back and she was on top of him.

"Am I too heavy?" she asked.

"Hell no."

"Are your hip and leg fine with me here?"

"Don't ever leave," he said, stroking her back.

She kissed him again, her sensitive nipples pressed against the wiry hair of his chest. Moaning, she licked down his chest to his abs, kissing every curve of his six-pack and down to his obliques. Kelly rubbed herself over his cock, sliding it between her breasts.

"There's a pretty sight," he rasped out.

"How about this one?" She licked up the entire length of him.

Trent's whole body twitched. Kelly liked that reaction so much, she did it again, this time with the flat of her tongue.

"Come here," he said, rifling through the box and pulling out a condom.

"Not yet." She took him deep in her mouth and he groaned.

His fingers tangled in her hair as she moved her head up and down.

"Fuck, that feels incredible," he whispered as she hollowed her cheeks and sucked him tight. "Come around and let me taste you too."

She let him slide out of her mouth with a wet pop. "Not this time," she said. "This time I want all your concentration on how I'm making you feel."

Sucking him back into her mouth, she went at him in earnest. The sliding sounds her mouth made on him were messy and erotic when it was mixed in with his cries of passion. His hips pulsed as he fought not to fuck her mouth and she admired his control. But she wanted to shred it. She had dreamed about doing this for too long to not give it everything she had. Faster she pulled at him, swirling her tongue down his length and across the head of his cock. When his fingers tightened on her hair, she knew she had him and swallowed him deep as he exploded with a surprised grunt that tore out of his throat and shook through his body.

"That's what I wanted," Kelly murmured as she kissed her way back up to his mouth.

"Let me show you what I want." Trent placed the condom in her hand. "Put that on for me. My hands are going to be busy."

He captured her lips again as he reached between her thighs. She rolled on her back and spread her legs, allowing his talented fingers to tickle through her slick folds.

"Uh," she grunted in surprise when he pinched her nipple at the same time he touched her clit. The condom dropped from her nerveless fingers as her thighs tried to trap his hand where it was. He rubbed her in slow circles, a gentle touch that was different from the sharp tugs on her nipple. His mouth swallowed more of her cries as he stroked her until she was frantic.

Kelly had to use both hands to get the condom over his cock and completely on. She writhed under his fingers, sparks of electric pleasure coursing through her. "Please, please," she whispered.

"Come first and I'll give you what you want," he said, with a dark chuckle. Sucking the tip of her nipple hard, he plunged his fingers inside her.

Clamping her thighs around his arm, she came so hard she saw stars. She didn't recognize the sounds coming out of her body. When she sagged in release, he pushed her thighs wide and sank his hot cock in deep. Clutching at his muscled ass, she kissed him as he fucked her with long slow strokes that slammed the futon frame back into the wall. The rhythm was breathtaking and she enjoyed the hard press of his body in hers. The friction of this thick cock rubbed all the right places. Kelly was powerless to stop her body from slamming up to meet his every thrust.

"You are so beautiful," he whispered, a fervent prayer. "I've wanted you like this for so very long."

"I need you. I need this."

He picked up the pace, rocking into her hard and fast. She swore the legs of the futon lifted off the ground with the force of his strokes. Wrapping herself around him, Kelly pressed as close as she could get. He was slick with perspiration and she was so close to coming, she could barely hold on. Her body arched as lightning strikes of pleasure overrode her brain, and she contorted as waves of joy thrummed through her. Kelly whispered mindless gasps of ecstasy and Trent pulsed against her until he, too, stiffened and found a dramatic release.

"Damn," he panted, too shaken up to move for a long moment. Sliding out of her, he dropped on his back with his arm over his eyes. "Hell…" He tried for more words, but lapsed until his breathing was under control. He disposed of the condom and then dragged her against him. Boneless, Kelly fought to keep her eyes open as her body molded against his. At some point, he managed to cover them with a blanket, but she fell asleep listening to the steady thud of his heart against her ear.

Chapter Twelve

TRENT WAS STILL having a hard time moving when Kelly slipped out of his bed in the wee hours of the morning. He managed to crack open one eye to watch her do a reverse striptease as she got dressed.

"Stay," he croaked out. "Stay until your father leaves for the cattle."

"That was an hour ago," she said, sitting on the side of the bed to pull on her boots.

"Come by with Alissa later. We can go to lunch."

"I'll see. It might be more toward the afternoon. I've got pictures to edit before I send them to the paper, and then I want to get some of them framed and see if any of the local boutiques will sell them on consignment."

"Okay," he said agreeably.

She kissed him. "Last night was wonderful."

"Come back tonight."

Her laugh was happy and it made him smile. "Greedy."

"You're lucky I'm still half asleep or you'd already be underneath me."

"Promises, promises." Kelly gave him a kiss that started waking up parts of him, but then it was over too quickly and she was gone.

Sated and lazy, he rolled over and slept until noon.

EVERY INCH OF his body ached. He barely made it down the stairs and into the shower. For some fortunate reason, the shower stall was installed with a seat and he was so very grateful for either his or Billy's foresight in doing that. He let the hot water drench him and felt his tight muscles ease. When he thought he would survive, Trent staggered out of the shower and gingerly got dressed. Maybe he'd overdone it last night with the horseback riding and the bullfighting and the lovemaking, but damn he'd do it all over again. Sign him up.

After washing some Tylenol down with his coffee, Trent got dressed and went outside to check on things. More packages had arrived. He'd bring them in when he was confident he could bend and get up again. Still, as he walked to the barn to check on Flower, he could definitely tell that he was walking better than he had been in a while. Maybe his body was healing more of the damage.

As he was walking back, he saw a cattle trailer pull in and back up to the paddock. What was Frank doing now? But Billy jumped out of the passenger side and Enrique Chavez got out of the driver's. Trent stopped walking, his eyes sliding to the trailer.

"What the hell is going on, Billy?" he asked. "Hiya, Enrique. Sorry, I didn't get a chance to talk with you last night."

"Open up the paddock," Billy said, coming over to him. "We're going to take some pictures with Corazon del Diablo."

Something flashed through him. Fear? Excitement? Hate? Trent covered it by asking, "How much is this costing me?"

"Considering a vial of sperm costs two grand, you probably don't want to know," Billy said, opening the paddock while Enrique went to the trailer door.

"You coming or what?" Enrique asked the bull in Spanish.

After a few moments, Corazon del Diablo sauntered down the ramp and into the paddock like he owned it.

Trent's jaw set and his fingers clenched into fists.

I could do it. I could ride him.

"I'll give you a million dollars to climb on his back right now," Chavez said, a gleam in his eyes.

"How long do I have to stay on?" Trent forced himself to relax and grin at the bull owner casually.

"No," Billy said. "No. No. That's not the type of pictures we want."

"Speak for yourself," Enrique said. "I've always regretted what happened. You would have been one of the greats."

That was one hell of a backward compliment. Trent just folded his arms and glared at the bull. The bull glared back. "What's this ornery bastard doing on my property?"

"We've got to start some buzz around you and the school," Billy said. "You did great last night, but now we have to keep up momentum. I figure with Enrique and his bull in town anyway, we can get some pictures taken and sent out to the media."

Kelly would be great at this. "I've got just the photographer in mind."

"We've got a reporter coming already," Enrique said.

Trent dialed Kelly's number anyway. When he got her voice mail, he texted her to call him about a photography job. While this was going on Enrique and Billy bickered like an old married couple, and Trent played stare-down with Corazon del Diablo. He wondered if the bull remembered him. If he was a bull, he'd remember every cowboy he'd stomped on.

A Jeep pulled up and the woman reporter from last night came out. She had a professional camera around her neck and a young boy with her. Trent looked over at Billy, but he shrugged.

Enrique smiled. "Ah, here she is. She's going to get us in the top country magazines in the world. I've worked with her before. She got my bulls into *Sports Illustrated* last year. Gentlemen, this is Lana Kirkland."

"Pleasure," Billy said, approaching her to shake her hand.

Trent didn't want to be rude, but he also didn't want to turn his back on the two-thousand-pound nightmare in his paddock. Leaning on the fencing, he eyed the bull warily, and the bull eyed him back. Maybe they had both gotten older and, hopefully, a little more mellow.

The boy joined him by the fence. "He looks mean."

"He is," Trent said. "What's your name?"

"Michael."

"Nice to meet you, Michael. I'm Trent."

"I know who you are. You're my dad."

"What?" Trent turned his back on the bull for that. He stared down at the boy, trying to find some resemblance. Was that his nose? His chin?

A camera flashed and Trent looked up to see Lana taking a picture. He racked his brain trying to remember her, but he couldn't. Sure, she looked familiar. "How old are you?"

"Ten."

Ten years ago, he had been twenty-one. Squinting at Lana, he remembered his birthday party in Brazil. There was a reporter there. He had slept with her. Had it been Lana? He stared at her as she talked with Billy. Maybe. Probably. Let's face it, if she'd been willing, he'd have done it. "I didn't know," Trent whispered. "Why didn't your mother tell me?"

"She said you didn't want me."

Trent whipped his head back to the child. Out of the corner of his eye, he saw Lana raise her camera again, but Enrique waylaid her. Steering her by the arm toward the bull, Enrique turned her focus to Corazon del Diablo.

"That's not true," Trent said.

"I didn't think so," Michael said. "She told me not to say anything, but I knew she was wrong."

Trent clamped a hand on the boy's shoulder. "I don't know why I wasn't told, but I'll make it up to you. I promise."

"I want to be a bull rider, like you. Will you teach me?"

"Of course...son. Of course." He racked his brain trying

to remember that night. He must have used a condom. But what if he hadn't? The private investigator Billy hired hadn't mentioned a Lana Kirkland. He should get him on the case, but he was all thumbs as he fumbled to text.

"Trent, get over here," Enrique said.

Fuck it. He'd do it later. He jammed his phone into his pocket and stalked over to Lana. "It's nice to see you again, Trent," she said.

"It's been a while," he said guardedly. "Cancun?"

"Rio de Janeiro."

Shit. He nodded. "Right."

There was an awkward pause and then Enrique butted in. "We don't have all day. Here, Trent. Get in there and let's get going."

"Get in there with him? Why? So he can chase me around?"

"He could care less until you try and get him in the chute."

Trent eyeballed the bull and then his owner. "Uh-huh."

But in the end, he went in. He wanted a closer look at the bull that had taken him out. Without the crowd cheering and jeering and the activity of the bull riders, Corazon del Diablo was content to meander around the pen, not paying Trent a damn bit of attention. As he approached the bull, Trent wondered what he'd do if the son of a bitch decided to charge. He eyed the distance to the sides of the paddock and figured he'd have a decent chance to make it.

Trent didn't remember the details of the pictures. He posed with his archrival and felt only numbness. He was still reeling about Michael's revelation. Trent had a son. And a daughter. How the hell was he going to support two kids when he wasn't pulling in PBR money anymore?

It was one thing to take a business risk when it was just him and Billy to worry about. Now, he had deeper responsibilities. Maybe even child support.

"Okay," Lana called. "Fold your arms and scowl at the bull."

"Seriously?"

"Play along," Billy called. "I like where she's going with this."

"For fuck's sake," he muttered under his breath.

The bull snorted as if to agree with him.

"We're both pretty much out to pasture, aren't we?" Trent said to the bull. "At least you get to go out a winner."

Squinting back at Michael, who was leaning on the paddock, Trent wondered if Michael saw a washed-up cowboy. Alissa was too young to remember his career, but Michael had probably followed him for a bit, before it ended. Before this bull ended it.

"Good," Lana called.

"We're just actors on the stage," Trent said, thinking back on the Shakespeare he'd practiced in rehab. "You have your part to play, and I have mine." He looked down at the bull. "You don't even know who I am. I bet you never even thought of me once you left the arena that night." He risked putting his hand on the bull's shoulder.

It shook him off with a threatening toss of his head, but didn't do anything more aggressive.

"You're not going to haunt me any longer."

Surprisingly enough, the bull didn't give a damn about being photographed as Lana called out other shots that she wanted to take. And true to Enrique's word, it was only when they wanted to put him in the chute that Corazon del Diablo started acting up. He had to jump away to avoid being kicked. "Back up," he told Michael, making sure the boy was standing in the studio platform above the pen, looking down into it. He didn't want Corazon del Diablo to think Michael was a rider about to hop on his back.

"One million dollars," Enrique called out. "You scared?"

Lana was furiously writing everything down. She barely looked up from her notepad. She had a recorder going, too.

"Your bull outweighs me by a good eighteen hundred pounds and bucks like the devil he's named after. Only an idiot wouldn't be cautious. But scared?" Trent shook his head, avoiding Billy and Enrique as they used ropes to get the bull into the chute. "I'm not eighteen anymore. My job isn't to ride Corazon del Diablo. It's to teach other riders how to stay on for eight seconds and get off without being hurt."

"Well, you know what they say," Enrique quipped. "Those who can't do, teach."

Trent resisted the urge to give him the finger. "Is that million dollars burning a hole in your pocket so badly that you're trying to trash-talk me into riding your bull again?"

"I'm dreaming of the money we'd make in Madison Square Garden."

"Well, keep dreaming," Billy said. "My boy is retired."

One million dollars. That would pay a lot of child support. And let him get one more chance to end his career on a high note. On a winning note. When the bull wouldn't settle down, they gave up and let him wander the pasture. They took the photo shoot inside, so Lana could get some interior shots of the school. He put Michael on the training machine and gave him a quick lesson.

He had always wanted children, and now he had two of them. The timing was weird, though. Why hadn't Lana told him about Michael years ago? She obviously knew how to find him. Billy must have scared her off as well. Trent sent off the text to the private investigator to see what he could turn up. It was probably going to have to come down to the DNA testing. "I'm thinking of hanging up Corazon del Diablo's harness. It would be a nice last ride for both of you."

"It would have been," Trent agreed, reluctantly. But he wasn't eighteen anymore. Or even thirty. He ached when he walked and his leg would never be the same. He owed it to Alissa and Michael to be thankful he could still walk. Trent couldn't run his school from a wheelchair. "I've got nothing but respect for your bull." It was true, too. He shook Enrique's hand.

Kelly and Alissa walked in. "Is that who I think it is out in the paddock?"

"Yes, and for God's sake keep holding Alissa's hand." Oh hell, how was he going to tell Kelly about Michael? Would she hate him? Especially since he was going to ask for both children to have DNA tests. He didn't want any surprises.

However, he would believe that they were both his kids until proven otherwise by lab results.

Billy's head whipped up and his eyes narrowed on Kelly and Alissa. Kelly glared back, her distaste for him apparent in every line of her body.

"I want to see the bull." Alissa tugged on Kelly's hand.

"From outside the paddock. Far away," Trent said.

"I'll make sure they're all right," Billy said, walking toward them.

"Billy," Trent warned.

"Thank you, Mr. King. That would be very nice of you," Kelly said with a vicious sweetness in her voice. Trent shrugged. Billy deserved whatever was about to come down on his head.

"Are we done with pictures, Miss Kirkland?" Enrique asked after Billy, Kelly, and Alissa had moved away.

"Yes, sir. I'll send them out to you as soon as I've gone over them."

"Excellent. Trent, if you change your mind, you know how to reach me. Give me a hand getting him back in the trailer?"

"Sure thing."

"Michael, why don't you go help too?" Lana said.

"Okay." Michael scurried outside.

"You stay clear of where I tell you," Trent said. Just because he and the bull had come to their own peace while taking pictures, that didn't mean he trusted the son of a bitch.

One million dollars to do something he'd do for free.

Trent shook his head. No. He had to be smart.

One million dollars would pay for his kids' college, and would probably cover any medical expenses he'd incur. One million dollars for eight seconds or less. That would set him up nicely. He might even be able to buy the Three Sisters Ranch outright with a large down payment. Kelly wouldn't have to worry about her father tossing her out ever again.

Corazon del Diablo trotted back up into the trailer, docile as a lamb—a two-thousand-pound lamb. Trent let out a breath when Enrique jumped up into the driver's seat. He approached him while the others went back into the studio.

"One million dollars if I agree to ride him again?" Trent asked as casually as he could.

"One million dollars if you sit on top of him in the chute in front of the arena I book."

"What if I don't stay on for the eight seconds?"

"One million dollars."

"What if I do?"

"One million dollars."

"One million dollars for getting on him. I want three million if I stay on him for eight seconds."

"I don't have that kind of money."

Trent patted the truck's door. "Take up a collection."

Squaring his shoulders, he walked back into the studio. Trent wasn't sure what he should expect, but Billy had set up the kids watching television and he was in his office with the two women. Trent considered chasing after Enrique. Suddenly, riding Corazon del Diablo didn't seem as daunting as walking into that office with the mothers of his two children.

In the fell clutch of circumstance
I have not winced nor cried aloud.
Under the bludgeonings of chance
My head is bloody, but unbowed.

The wisp of poetry whispered across his brain.

Trent walked in and closed the door to the office behind him, so the children couldn't hear them. He could still see them watching television through the window, and a pang of longing went through him. Those were his kids. He had lost so much time. They had lost so much time, not knowing they each had a half sibling. He should have been more careful. This was all his fault.

He should have expected his carousing ways to come back to bite him on the ass someday. But he never, in a million years, thought that kids' lives would have been affected by it. He was damn sure going to make it up to them every day for the rest of his life. Riding Corazon del Diablo was just the start of what he was willing to do for them.

"I've been having an interesting conversation with Miss Sullivan and Miss Kirkland," Billy said.

Trent looked down, but Kelly was refusing to look at him. Her fists were clenched and her jaw was tight. Lana was staring up at him fearfully. He sighed and hitched a hip on his desk. "Let me guess. You asked Kelly for a cheek swab from Alissa for a DNA paternity test and Lana overheard and said that Michael was my son."

"What?" Billy snapped.

"What?" Kelly's head whipped up.

Oh shit.

"What were you guys talking about?" he asked hoarsely.

"That you were a damned fool if you were thinking of riding Corazon del Diablo again."

Fuck a duck.

"Excuse me," Kelly shot to her feet and bolted outside.

"Son of a bitch," he sighed, watching Kelly fetch Alissa. She almost had to drag the little girl out, kicking and screaming. He gave his daughter a wave.

"Boy, you have all the tact of Mexican fighting bull," Billy said.

"Apparently."

Lana rose up on shaky legs. "You knew Michael was your son? All these years and you never said a word? I had given you the benefit of the doubt. I thought he stonewalled me and kept the information from you." She pointed at Billy. "I figured, though, he did it under your orders. But there was a part of me that thought if you knew you had a son, you would have tried to see him once in ten years."

"No, I didn't know. Michael told me an hour ago, as we were looking at the bull."

"Oh." She sank back down into her chair. "Well, what do we do now?"

"Before we do anything, we swab Michael's cheek and Trent's cheek and wait for the results," Billy said. "We might as well do Alissa's too, since you mentioned it. I'll go get the kits if Miss Kirkland would be so kind as to drive me back to the Bluebonnet Inn."

"Sure." Lana stood up again. "I actually would like to interview you about the school, Trent. But it can wait." She opened the office door. "Michael, come on. We're leaving."

"Trent is going to teach me how to ride," he said, smiling wide.

"That's great." She glanced back at Trent and lowered her voice. "I'm sorry. This wasn't how I planned it to go."

"How did you plan it?"

"Over time. The interview would take several sessions where you could see him and get to know him and then, at the last one, he'd be with my mother and I would have told you that you were his father."

"I wish you'd told me ten years ago."

"I tried."

Trent nodded. "Billy didn't make it easy for anyone to get close to me, but you had my number, didn't you?"

She shook her head. "We didn't get that far. It wasn't meant to last more than one crazy night in Rio."

"Has he been…has he had a good life, growing up without a father?" Trent asked the question that he feared the answer to the most.

"The best," Lana said. "He's been smothered with love since the day he was born."

Trent blinked back the emotion flooding through him. "Good. That's good."

She touched his arm. "I've always told him the truth about you. He knew about your accident and when he found out you were making an appearance in Last Stand's rodeo, he begged me to go. I should have known he would find a way to tell you before I did."

"Mom, come on," Michael called from the doorway.

Laughing shakily, Lana nodded and tossed Michael the keys. "I'll be right there. Get in the car and turn on the air conditioner."

"What do you want from me?" Trent asked.

"Nothing you're not willing to give. But if you don't want anything to do with Michael, please let him down easy."

"If he is my son, I want to be a part of his life."

"Are you married?" she asked.

"Girlfriend. Kelly. The one who ran out of here."

Lana winced. "I'm sorry."

"It was my big mouth that caused this. I'll find a way to smooth it over. Somehow," he said, bleakly.

"Let me know if I can do anything to help." Lana stood up on her tiptoes and gave him a quick kiss. "And stay off that damned bull."

Chapter Thirteen

THE PATERNITY TEST results hadn't come back yet, but Kelly wasn't worried. Not about Alissa anyway. She was worried about Lana and Michael. Each time she went to see Trent, he was out somewhere.

Sure, he asked Kelly to stay while Lana continued with the alleged interview she was doing. Lana was giving Trent what he wanted—time with his child. It was what Kelly should have been doing. Luckily, she had more than enough work to do to keep her occupied.

Her baby sister, Emily, had finally breezed in one morning during breakfast and was currently the focus of her father's attention, thankfully. Emily had another idea to help put the farm into the black. Her newest obsession was wind turbines and she was pressuring him to buy ten of them. According to her, that could bring in eighty thousand dollars a year for the next thirty-five years. Her father was skeptical, but Emily was going to drown him in case studies until he capitulated. Of course, it wasn't that simple. They had to find a developer to come in and see if they even had the wind speeds coming through the land to make it a viable option. But when Emily was on fire, you either went with it or waited until something else caught her attention.

Kelly and Janice were out in the southern part of the ranch every day with the Sykes Construction crew, building the retreat cabin and formulating plans. The crew had even been nice enough to put her cheap gazebo and pavilion together.

Today, Emily had joined them in painting the gazebo and pavilion white. Aunt Candace's bride was flying in at the end of the week on her private jet to take a look at the place. Kelly wanted everything set up and ready to impress her.

Emily wanted to finish the job quickly so they could ride around the ranch in the truck, looking for possible areas to start a wind farm. Kelly didn't know how she thought they could afford the turbines, but maybe her time with the Peace Corps had given her some contacts with environmental grants.

While they worked, Kelly decided that now was as good a time as any to tell them about Trent. She wasn't sure how to start, but luckily Janice asked one of her nosy questions.

"Why haven't we seen Trent around lately? Did you two have a fight?"

"Not exactly." Kelly put down her brush. "I've wanted to tell you guys this for a long time, but I just couldn't. Now that we're all here, I'm telling you two first."

"Spit it out already," Emily said. Her waist-length hair was tied in a long braid down her back. Kelly resisted the urge to tug her off the ladder by it.

Shrugging, she figured she might as well get it over with. "Trent is Alissa's father."

"What?" Janice steadied Emily when the ladder wobbled.

"Does he know?" Emily asked.

"He does now. He never knew I was pregnant. He never got my calls, and his manager never gave him my messages. I told him a few weeks ago. It was the first time I'd seen him again since that night when he got a ninety-five on Fire-cracker."

"Do Mom and Dad know?" Janice said, biting her nail before she realized it was covered in paint. She spit out paint and wiped her mouth.

"No. I haven't broken the news to them yet."

"Why not?" Emily asked.

"I wasn't sure of Trent. I wasn't sure how Dad would react. And now, it seems I'm not the only one Trent impreg-nated."

"Shut the front door," Emily said. "Do we need to go over there with some pitchforks?"

"No, it happened five years before he met me."

"You shouldn't have kept this a secret," Janice said. "Not from us. We wouldn't have judged you."

"It didn't matter," Kelly said. "I was wrong when I thought he'd ghosted me, and that he didn't want Alissa. And now while we're waiting for the paternity test results, I feel so guilty. This should be a done deal and he should already have a relationship with Alissa."

"You've done nothing wrong," Emily said, climbing down the ladder and hugging her fiercely.

"Intellectually, I know that. But all I want to do is cry."

Janice joined in the group hug. "How is Trent reacting

to all this?"

"He's busy getting ready for his grand opening. He's got mutton busters and middle schoolers and a few high schoolers lined up. He's even booked a one-on-one training session. And when he's not busy he's with Lana, the possible mother of his other child. He's teaching Michael."

"That says absolutely nothing about how he feels about you and Alissa," Emily said.

"I'm afraid to ask him."

"What's changed?" Janice asked, all "voice of reason" in her posture. Meanwhile, Emily was looking around for weapons.

"Alissa has a half brother. Maybe. I think I need to know for sure before I can move on from this. Right now, I'm just glad we're keeping busy."

They looked up when a Range Rover approached, going at a fast clip. Emily groaned. "Not this guy again."

It parked next to the Sykes Construction trucks and a handsome man in an orange safety vest and camouflage pants stepped out of it. He went around to the other side and opened the door for their mother and Alissa.

"That has to be Donovan Link," Kelly mused.

"Unfortunately," Emily said. "I'm surprised he's not wearing a hat with deer antlers on it."

"I'd bet he'd have a nice rack," Janice joked.

Donovan was fine to look at, but there was something about him that made you think he wasn't going to steal your wallet, but he knew where it was.

"Mommy!" Alissa came running up to her.

"You're going to get paint all over you." But Kelly picked her up and put her on her hip. Every day she was getting bigger and, pretty soon, Kelly wasn't going to be able to pick her up anymore. Suddenly, it was all too much. Trent had a right to share moments like this with his daughter. She should be there, alongside Lana and Michael, if need be. Otherwise, she could lose him to his new family.

"Hey, guys, I need to take a break. Give me a call when you want me to come and pick you up."

"Where are you going?" her mother said. "I wanted to introduce you to Donovan."

"Hi," Kelly said, holding her hand out. "Sorry about the paint."

"Not a problem." He flashed her a killer smile and she couldn't help but smile back. "I was hoping to take a look around. Your mom said one of you could give me a tour."

"Emily can do it," Janice volunteered. "We were just heading back to the ranch and she wanted to look for spots for the wind turbines."

"What about the painting? That's not going to finish itself," Emily complained.

But Kelly had already buckled Alissa into her car seat in their rental car. Janice eased in next to Alissa, and her mother took the passenger seat.

"He's such a nice man," her mother said. "I'm hoping he can make Emily see reason."

"That's a recipe for disaster," Janice said, peering out the window at them. "I think they're arguing already."

"Your sister means well, but she doesn't think things

through."

"She has her own way of doing things, Mom. That doesn't mean she's wrong." Kelly felt the need to defend Emily—even if her mother's feelings reflected her own.

Kelly dropped her mother and sister off at the ranch house and drove up to the studio.

"Where are we going, Mommy?" Alissa asked.

"We're going to spend some time with Trent."

THE BULL-RIDING SCHOOL didn't have enough room for them to hang out and relax. So, after Alissa had her fill of riding on Flower and they'd finished their chores, Trent suggested they head over to the Bluebonnet Inn where they could use Billy's key to swim in the pool.

The water was bathtub warm, but it was fun to do a few laps. Kelly was thrilled to see Alissa and Trent horsing around in the water. Alissa would splash him and he'd pick her up and toss her. Kelly gave up on trying to keep her hair dry, and by the time hunger chased them out of the pool, she was almost yawning as hard as Alissa.

They came back to the school after a quick food shopping trip. Trent grilled up hotdogs for Alissa and a steak for the two of them. She made a Caesar salad since that was the only green food Alissa would eat, although she ate more croutons than lettuce. But Kelly took it as a win.

When Alissa went for a second handful of chips, Kelly stopped her. "You've had enough."

"Just three more?" She turned sad puppy dog eyes on Trent.

"Maybe, just three?" he suggested.

Kelly raised an eyebrow at him and, thankfully, he backed down.

"Your mom said no."

Alissa scowled.

"Keep it up and no dessert," she said.

Since dessert was a scoop of vanilla ice cream in between two chocolate chip cookies, Alissa decided to pick her battles, and finished all her salad instead of asking for more chips.

Once everything was cleaned up, they headed back to the ranch house where Alissa demanded a bedtime story from Trent. Her sisters fell over themselves and giggled when they saw the three of them together. They were terrible actresses and Kelly knew she was going to have to tell her father soon, because they were going to give it away with their antics.

She practically had to slap Emily's phone out of her hand because she kept taking pictures of Trent and Alissa together. Her father seemed out of it. He was still recovering from the long hours on the trail. But her mother kept giving them all curious looks. It was a ticking time bomb, and she knew she had to come out and tell everyone. But first, she wanted to know about Michael and Lana. After Alissa was tucked in, she and Trent took a bottle of wine and sat on the porch swing together.

"Today was nice," he said, kissing her forehead. "Thank you for that."

Emily giggled and took a picture of them on the swing.

"I'm going to shove that phone somewhere unpleasant," Kelly warned.

The porch door slammed shut.

"Is that what having siblings is like?"

"Unfortunately," Kelly said.

They swung a bit, sipping their wine. "Any word about the test results?"

"No, I'd tell you. And I will, as soon as I hear. I just want you to know, there's no doubt in my mind that Alissa is my daughter."

"Shhh," she said.

"Your father was snoring his fool head off in the recliner and your mother is still upstairs."

"Still," Kelly said. "This is not how I want them to find out."

"I've been patient, Kelly. It's time to tell them."

"Let's get the tests out of the way first."

"Why? Is there a doubt?" he asked agitated.

"No, don't be an idiot. I was only with you. I was thinking more of Lana and Michael. If we're going to rock my family's world with the news you're her father, I'd rather tell them at the same time that she has a half brother."

"I guess that makes sense." Trent stared broodingly into his wineglass.

"Unless you're sure about Michael, too."

"I'm not as sure about Michael," he admitted.

"Why?"

"I don't remember every woman I've ever been with, that's true. You were unforgettable." He brushed a stray lock of hair that had slipped out of her ponytail behind her ear. "I didn't remember sleeping with Lana at first. But after I thought about it, I did. I also remembered that I wasn't the only one she was with in Rio de Janeiro."

Kelly straightened up so fast, the swing jerked and she almost sloshed wine on herself. "Did you tell her that?"

He shook his head. "There's no point in it. The tests will prove if Michael is my son or not."

"But you've been spending so much time with them. Isn't he going to be disappointed if the test is negative?"

"I'm sure he will be at first, but this will allow him to find his real dad. Frankly, I don't think Lana was very interested in finding out who it was or she would have done this sooner. I think me and my big mouth escalated the situation. Besides…" He kicked back so they were rocking slowly again. "Michael is still going to attend my school. It's not like I'm going to kick him to the curb, just because he's another man's son, if that's the case. Billy didn't turn me away and I want to pay that forward."

"You're a good man," she said, leaning her head on his shoulder.

"Yeah, but I'm not a very patient one."

"Soon." Kelly linked her fingers through his. "What's another week or so?"

"Have you figured out the best way to tell your father? Because he's going to be the hard one, from what you said."

"We do it as a family. Me, you, Alissa and my sisters."

"He's not going to feel ganged up on?"

"Trust me. There's safety in numbers."

"Are you going to come see me tonight?" he breathed in her ear, and nibbled at her earlobe.

"I'd love to, but I can't. I promised Janice and Emily I'd go on the cattle drive with them tomorrow."

Trent winced. "Don't you have ranch hands to do that?"

"Yes, but my father made a sexist remark to Emily and now we all have to suffer for it. Besides, Janice thinks this might be a great event to add to her women's retreat."

"What does Nate think of this?"

"I don't repeat language like that." Kelly giggled.

Chapter Fourteen

T RENT WATCHED THE last of prospective students drive
away, their parents' cars kicking up dust and putting
grooves in the smooth dirt. The open house had been a big
success, but he was going to have to come up with some
money to pave a parking lot before Frank saw the mess the
cars were making of his land.

The buzz of an ATV caught his attention. Speak of the
devil, here he was. Squinting, Trent looked to see if Alissa
was with him. Kelly and her sisters would be out with the
cattle until lunchtime, but Alissa was staying with her
grandparents. Unfortunately, Frank seemed to be alone. At
least, Trent didn't have to haul Flower out. The poor sheep
was pooped. He might have to buy another one so they
could alternate days.

Kelly had gotten some really cute pictures of Alissa riding
Flower and he couldn't wait to put them up in the studio.

"You son of a bitch," Frank snarled when he got into
earshot.

"Excuse me?" What the hell had gotten into him?

Trent jumped back onto the paddock because Frank was
coming in fast and angry like a bull on that ATV and he

didn't think he was going to stop. But he did, hitting the brakes hard enough that the machine spun in a circle. Confused, Trent hopped down and walked over to him.

Red-faced, Frank rushed at Trent, swinging wildly. "I'll kill you, you bastard."

"Frank." Trent dodged and stepped away. Frank chased after him, swinging and hollering insults and threats. "What is going on?"

"She told me. She told me."

Oh hell. Jeez, Kelly, a little warning. "I would have liked to have been there when she did."

"I bet you would have. You coward." Winded, Frank bent over and put his hands on his knees. "If I'd have known, I never would have had you on this ranch."

"I'm sorry this has upset you. Kelly should have made it clear that I…" Trent stopped. What if Frank was pissed about the bull or something else? He didn't want to make the same mistake twice. "Wait, what are we talking about?"

"As if you didn't know." Frank was gulping air, his sides heaving from exertion.

"Why don't you come inside? Have a cold drink and we can discuss this like men."

"Don't talk to me about men. Where were you when my baby was pregnant?"

Something snapped inside Trent. Where was he? Was this guy for real? "I didn't know she was pregnant. But where the fuck were you?"

It was like he'd waved a red T-shirt in front of Corazon del Diablo. Frank put his head down and charged. Trent didn't want to do this, but he wasn't going to have the old man chase him around the pen. At the last minute, he put to use the skills he'd learned when bullfighting as a boy, and stepped aside, giving Frank a hard shove.

Frank went down to his hands and knees. Spit dribbled out of his mouth. "You think you're so tough, picking on an old man."

Trent wasn't proud of shoving Kelly's father, but it was in self-defense. "You came out here and attacked me in my place of business."

"This is my land," Frank roared. "I want you off it."

Frank's face was turning purple.

Trent had to calm him down. This was getting way out of hand. "I have a lease. I'm not going anywhere. Now, I'm not sure what the hell Kelly told you…"

"Kelly didn't tell me a goddamned thing. She's next." Frank stayed on the ground, his breathing becoming more ragged.

"Frank, I'm worried about you. Let's go inside and sit down."

"Shove your worry up your ass."

"You're acting crazy irrational. Why don't you tell me what's gotten you so riled up?"

"I was leading my sweet, angelic granddaughter on her pony and she says to me, 'I know who my daddy is.' So, I ask who, thinking she's going to tell me it's some TV star. She tells me it's you. Then she tells me she has a brother."

"I don't know where she got that information." Trent wasn't going to deny it, but he wasn't sure Frank was thinking clearly enough right now to lie.

"She said she overheard you talking last night."

Trent took a deep breath. What if that hadn't been Emily at the door giggling? What if it had been Alissa? "Where is she now?"

"Her grandmother has her. I was too mad to think clearly. I plucked her off the pony and handed her to Sarah and came straight here."

Trent hunkered down so they were eye-to-eye. "What were you hoping to accomplish?"

"I was going to beat the ever-loving shit out of you for leaving my daughter in the lurch."

"I only just found out Alissa was my daughter a few weeks ago."

"You treated my daughter like she was a floozy."

"My relationship with your daughter is none of your business, but you better watch your mouth when you're talking about the woman I love."

"Love? Get the hell off my ranch or I'll come back here with a shotgun and force you out."

"You come back here with a shotgun and I'll throw your ass in jail."

"If I was thirty years younger, you'd be eating your teeth right now."

"You don't have to like me, Frank. But I am Alissa's father. And I'm going to be in her life. I might even be your son-in-law someday, so let's end this right now. Forget it ever happened and go on."

"I'll never forgive you," he said.

"For what? A five-year misunderstanding that I'll spend the rest of my life making up for gladly? Fine. I don't need your forgiveness. But I need you to get up, put your big girl panties on and deal with it." Trent held out his hand to help him up and Frank slapped it away.

"I didn't speak to my daughter for two years," Frank growled between ragged breaths.

"Well, whose fault is that? I wouldn't talk to you either if you kicked me out when I needed you most. Did you tell her you'd never forgive her, either?"

"She should have told me. She should have trusted me."

"When you act like this? Why the hell should she?"

"Because I'm her father, damn it."

"Maybe she should have told you," Trent reasoned. "But she didn't. And there's nothing that can change that. So, let's shake hands and go on from here."

"You need to get off my property."

"If you want me off the property I signed a legal lease for, then you're going to need a really good attorney. Because I'm not going anywhere."

Frank coughed. "This ranch isn't going to last the three years of that lease. I've got creditors coming out of the woodwork, but I'll see you out of here before I have to sell."

"I wouldn't underestimate your daughters. They're smart women. They'll find a way to save this ranch, in spite of you."

Grimacing in pain, Frank hauled himself up to his feet. "You're going to do right by my little girl."

"That's between her and me."

"Who is this brother Alissa was talking about? Did you knock up some buckle bunny?" He made a face of distaste.

"That's none of your business. And I think you should leave."

Frank swayed and glared at him. "You think you can throw me off my own land? You're going to have to knock me out and toss me in the ATV."

"Don't tempt me, Frank."

He gave a half laugh and rubbed at his face. "I was your biggest fan. I went to every rodeo. I memorized your stats. I knew which bull you were going to ride before you did, probably."

"It's eight seconds on a bull. It doesn't make me someone to worship or emulate." Trent realized the irony in what he was saying. He'd been knocking himself around for not ending his career on a high note. The high note was he was alive and had a daughter and a beautiful woman he'd someday like to make his wife. He didn't need one last ride or a million dollars. He had everything he needed. Now, if he could only make Frank Sullivan see reason.

"I wanted to be you. And then it turns out you knocked up my daughter and left her without another word. Even if you didn't know she was pregnant, you never called her again. I want to kill you for making her feel like that."

Trent ground his teeth. He knew the feeling. He'd like to kill Frank for making Kelly doubt herself, and after all these years, feel she had to earn her way back into her father's good graces. His daughter would never have to do that. "I lost my phone. There were miscommunications and then I was hospitalized and in rehab for most of my daughter's life. I wouldn't have left them in the lurch. I wouldn't have thrown my six-months-pregnant daughter out of my house. You want someone to beat up or to blame for Kelly's pain?" Trent leaned in close. "Look in the fucking mirror."

Frank lunged for him and this time, Trent let him get in a punch. It was a solid one that rocked his head back and stung like a bitch. But it made his decision to retaliate easier. Trent cocked back his fist to show Frank the error of his ways, when Frank's eyes suddenly rolled back in his head.

"Frank?"

His body convulsed. His knees buckled. He hit the ground before Trent could catch him.

"Frank?"

No response.

"Fuck." Fumbling with his phone, Trent dropped it and cursed again. He scrambled to pick it up and dialed for help.

"Nine, one, one. What is your emergency?"

"I've got an old man flat out in the dirt in front of me. I think he had a heart attack. Send someone right away." Trent rattled off the address and then tossed the phone aside.

Starting CPR, he prayed he wouldn't have to tell Kelly her father died after he found out Trent was Alissa's dad.

"Don't you die, you stubborn bastard." He did chest compressions to "*Stayin' Alive*" by the BeeGees, because he'd once heard that matching the beats to the song was the best way to keep up a rhythm until the paramedics got there. "Kelly will never forgive herself. And Alissa still needs her pawpaw." Sweat gathered under his hat and dripped into his eyes. His back and legs were cramping, but he didn't stop.

Christ, did he have to go toe to toe with the old man? Couldn't he have taken the high road and let him rant and then calm down? No, he had to argue with him. He didn't have anything to justify to Frank Sullivan. He should have kept his cool.

The July heat beat down on his neck and he was starting to get tired. His arms shook. "Breathe, damn it." After what seemed an eternity, Trent heard the sirens in the distance, but he didn't stop the compressions, not even when the ambulance pulled in and screeched to a dusty stop.

"We got it from here," a paramedic said, as they rushed over.

His hands cramping and spasming, Trent tried to get up off the ground and couldn't. His damned knee had locked up. The paramedics had to help him up. "You all right?"

"Better than him," Trent said. "Is he going to be all right?"

"Are you his family?"

"No." Not yet.

"Better let them know to meet us at the hospital."

Wincing, Trent straightened up. Where the hell was his phone? And what the hell was he going to tell his daughter about her pawpaw?

Chapter Fifteen

KELLY PULLED INTO Trent's studio after spending all day at the hospital. Alissa was there helping with chores, but she came running like she always did when she saw her. Kelly hugged her tight because she needed it. They both did.

"Is PawPaw coming home today?" she asked, like she'd asked every day for the past two weeks.

"Not yet, sweetie. We hope soon." In addition to the second heart attack, he had fractured his hip when he fell. It was going to be a long recovery and he wouldn't be riding a horse for cattle drives anytime soon. Her mother said he was going to use a pickup truck. Nate was going to have his hands full keeping him out of trouble.

"Hey," Trent said, coming over to her and giving her a kiss.

She clung to him, determined not to cry in front of Alissa.

"Alissa, want to go watch some TV?"

"I'll go get Flower."

"Wait," Kelly said. "Flower can't come inside."

But Alissa ran upstairs.

"I got her a stuffed sheep," Trent said, with an embarrassed smile.

And sure enough, Alissa thundered back down the stairs carrying a white fluffy sheep with a pink bow.

She had a million stuffed animals, but Kelly couldn't bring herself to scold him. After all, it was the first stuffed animal he'd ever bought her. And it appeared to be her new favorite.

She knew Trent would go pop some popcorn, while Kelly set Alissa up on the mats in front of the television. The popcorn and her programs would keep Alissa distracted while they went into his office and talked. And they needed to talk.

After Alissa was content, Trent handed Kelly a glass of wine when she closed the office door behind her. She took it gratefully. She was bone tired and exhaustion battled with despair. Why had she let her life get so complicated?

"How's Frank?" he asked.

"Still not talking to me."

"I don't know why you keep going up there. You shouldn't let him treat you like that."

Kelly held out her palm to stop him right there. "He's my father."

"That doesn't give him carte blanche to abuse you."

"It's not abuse."

"It's bordering on it."

"Butt out," she said, louder than she'd meant to. It was complicated. She knew he was right, but she was too tired to fight about it. It was over. Her father's medical bills were the final nail in their financial coffin. Her parents would lose the ranch—all because she hadn't told her father about Trent when she should have. "It wasn't always like this, you know. I mean he always had a short temper, but he only started getting really nasty after his first heart attack. I keep remembering happier times when he would tease us and we could tease him back. I wish I didn't have to see him suffer and be in pain."

There was a tense silence for a few minutes and then Trent said, "I got the paternity reports back today."

"What did they say?" She couldn't be more disinterested. It didn't matter. All her careful plans about easing her father in to the truth had exploded when she hadn't noticed Alissa eavesdropping on their conversation. Of course, there was a chance her father would have still acted the same way. Only in that situation, he would have done it in front of everyone, Alissa included. At least finding out the way he did, it had saved Alissa the heartbreak of watching her pawpaw break down.

"Alissa's my daughter," Trent said.

"Yes, I'm aware of that." She stared into her wine. He wasn't going to like what she was going to tell him, yet there was no way she couldn't face the situation head on.

"Michael is not my son."

The hurt in his voice caused her to look up. The relief she felt shamed her. She hadn't wanted to share him with another woman, but there was a little boy who'd just lost a father. "Are you okay?"

"Yeah, nothing's going to change. I told that to Lana and Michael. He's a great kid and he could use a father figure."

"I'm glad," she said, and meant it. That was one good outcome for today.

"And I sent in my DNA samples to a bunch of different databases. I'm going to try and find my father."

"You are?"

Trent shrugged one shoulder. "It's a long shot. But seeing Michael looking so lost and remembering how that felt, I started to wonder who my father is again, too."

"You're welcome to mine."

"Thanks," he said sarcastically.

"What do you know about him?" Kelly said.

"Not much. He was a bullfighter. She followed him around for a season."

"Did Billy know him?"

"No." Trent smirked. "My mother slept around. Billy doesn't like telling me that. Like I have a leg to stand on in the judgment department."

"Don't." She put her hand on his arm. "There's no judgment. You were both young and sowing wild oats."

"Yeah, well it seemed we sowed a bit more than oats." Trent looked out the window of his office to Alissa.

"Well, I hope you find what you're looking for." She finished her wine and poured herself another glass.

"You seem more down than usual. Is there something more than your father bothering you?"

And there it was. She wanted to delay telling him, but if she learned nothing from her father's meltdown, it was not to sit on important information. "I'm going back to New York."

"You can't." Trent stared at her, dumbstruck.

She shook her head sadly. "I don't have a choice."

"You're giving up on the photo studio? I thought that rich chick loved the sample photos you took."

"He kicked me out. Again."

Trent closed his eyes. "I don't understand why."

"For lying to him."

"What purpose does that serve now?"

"It's a pride thing, I think. He's embarrassed and angry and this is how he reacts."

"And your mother is on board with this?"

"Surprisingly, this time she isn't. Although, I'm not sure I trust that completely. She says she's on my side. So are my sisters. But they don't want to upset him while he's recovering, so I think it's best that Alissa and I just go back to New York."

"Best for who?"

Kelly paced the small office, draining her second glass of wine in one grateful gulp. She wanted to feel calm and sleepy, but it wasn't working. Instead her stomach gurgled and she tasted fire in the back of her throat. "There's no point in staying. His medical bills are going to finish the ranch. Even if Emily gets her field of wind turbines, we're not going to keep the creditors at bay long enough to see any of our projects take off. You and Donovan are the lucky ones. Build up your school roster and then relocate somewhere that's yours."

"I like it here. We've made a few memories here."

Kelly blushed. "We can make more. Just in New York."

"Stay here with me. This is where you belong."

"Here? There's not enough room for all three of us."

"Then we'll rent an apartment or buy a condo."

She wished she could do that. She wished it was that easy. It was too soon and there was so much she had to think of. If it had just been her and not Alissa, Kelly would have jumped at the chance to live with him. But what if it all went up in flames? She had to protect Alissa's feelings. "I love you, Trent, but I'm not ready for that yet."

He took in a shuddering breath. "That's the first time you've ever said that to me. Why does it sound like goodbye?"

"Because it is. I'm never coming back here again. After this week, I'll probably never even see my father again. And he's going to die, disappointed in me." Her voice broke and the next thing she knew, she was sobbing in his arms. Kelly had wanted to be strong, but at least Alissa couldn't see her breaking down like this. She had to pull it together, but right now she needed Trent to comfort her and help her get through this. "All my life, I wanted to be his perfect little girl. But I couldn't."

"No one could live up to what he wanted." Trent stroked her back and kissed her head. "Do you want me to talk to him?"

She hiccupped against his shirt. "Do you want him to have another heart attack?"

He stiffened under her hands. "Does your family blame me?"

"No, no. I was making a dumb joke. You're not the first

person he lost his temper about. Thank you for not pressing charges against him for assaulting you."

"Well if he hadn't had a heart attack right there in front of me, I probably would have assaulted him back. I still might," Trent added. "Stay." He cupped her cheek and tilted her head so she looked up at him.

"I don't want to be here when he gets out. I don't want to subject Alissa to that. I've booked our flight back for the end of the week."

"That soon? Why didn't you talk this over with me before you bought the tickets?"

"There's nothing to say."

"And if I want my daughter here with me?"

A muscle worked in her jaw. "Trent, don't do this to me. Not now." She couldn't take one more thing going wrong.

"What about what you're doing to me?" He tried to take her back into his arms, but she moved away. "Frank may be discharged out of the hospital soon, but they're going to put him in rehab for his hip for a few months. Emily told me and Donovan a few days ago.

"I need to get back to my life and stop chasing this silly dream of saving the Three Sisters Ranch. I need to make my own dream of having my own business come true."

"There's nothing you can't do here that you'd be doing in New York. Stay. Forget your father. Stay for me and for Alissa."

"There are too many bad memories in that ranch house for me to stay, whether he's there or not."

"Then stay here with me or at the Bluebonnet Inn. We

can even go a few towns over."

"I need some space, Trent." She needed to lick her wounds and recover from her father's latest insanity. Anger simmered inside her. How dare he kick her off the ranch, when she'd dropped everything to come here and save it?

"Then leave Alissa here with me until you figure things out."

She gasped. "I can't do that. She barely knows you."

"Her aunts and grandmother are right next door." Trent jerked his thumb in the direction of the ranch house.

"Her home is with me."

"She has two homes now. Wherever you are and wherever I am."

"How can you be so cruel as to take her away from me?" Kelly cried out, wiping furiously at the tears that rolled down her cheeks.

"I could ask you the same question." His face was sad, but stoic.

"Do what you have to do, Trent." She stormed out of his office, slamming the door. "Let's go," she said, hauling up Alissa, not caring that the popcorn spilled all over the floor.

"Noooo," Alissa complained. "I want to stay."

Kelly's broken heart shattered into a million pieces, but she didn't let Alissa go. Once they were in the car driving back to the house, Kelly tried to keep it together. This was for the best. Or was it? Hell, she didn't know what she wanted, anymore. But it wasn't this.

Chapter Sixteen

TRENT SAT IN his office drinking the rest of the bottle of wine before switching to whiskey. By the time his glass was empty, he had already made his decision. He called up Enrique Chavez and hoped he wasn't slurring his words.

"Have you got my purse money yet?" he asked as a conversation starter.

Enrique was ready for him. "If you wear patches on your vest of a few of my handpicked sponsors during every interview you do and during the ride, you get your three million dollars—if you go the full eight seconds. Otherwise, you get one million."

That would have to be enough. "I'll have Billy call you to iron out the details."

"It's good to have you back, Trent."

Three million dollars for eight seconds.

Billy was going to kill him.

Chapter Seventeen

KELLY WAS IN the waiting room of the hospital playing Chutes and Ladders with Alissa and another little boy who was there with his father. She wasn't sure why she bothered coming in. Her father still refused to see her. She glanced at her phone, hoping Trent would return her messages. He'd stopped answering his phone. Kelly wondered if he really was ghosting her this time. She wanted to see him one last time before she left for New York. She wanted to make it right.

She was going to offer him school vacations and then all summer, as long as she was there too. Kelly knew it wasn't ideal, but it was the best she could do. They could FaceTime every day. But in her heart, she knew if the situation was reversed, she would be wretched. She didn't know how to fix this.

Emily burst through the waiting room doors, her eyes wide and panicked. Fear slammed Kelly's heart against her rib cage. "Get in there," she said. "I'll stay here with Alissa."

Emily gave her a quick hug as she rushed past. Kelly didn't know what to expect, but when she rushed into the hospital room, her father scowled at her. "Get out. And turn this shit off."

No one was paying attention to him. Janice was riveted to the television set, her hand over her mouth. Her mother was staring at Trent on ESPN. He was wearing full bull-riding gear as he spoke to Lana.

"What's going on?" Kelly asked.

"I said turn this shit off," her father grumbled.

"Shh," Janice said and raised the volume.

"Are you sure your body is recovered enough to get back on a bull? And not just any bull, but Corazon del Diablo," Lana said, her perfect face taut and unsmiling.

"I can do anything for eight seconds."

"Oh no." Kelly sank into a chair. "What's that crazy idiot doing?"

"Shh," Janice said.

"What brought you out of retirement?" Lana looked about as happy as Kelly felt. Her lips were tightly pressed together and she was tense.

Trent, on the other hand, was all good-old-boy charm. "A lot of things. This is going to be Corazon del Diablo's last ride. I've arranged for a few perks for myself and my family if I can stay on his back for eight seconds."

"Like what?"

"Ernesto Chavez is going to give me some sperm for my breeding stocks."

"What breeding stocks?" Frank grumbled despite himself.

"You're going to raise bulls now?" Lana asked.

"I've got a bull-riding school and I plan on being there

for a long time."

"The hell you will," Frank muttered.

"I might as well see about raising some bulls for my future students to challenge themselves on."

"What are you going to do with the three-million-dollar purse if you manage to go eight seconds on the bull who ended your career five years ago?"

"I'm going to buy a cattle ranch in my hometown of Last Stand, Texas."

Janice turned off the television.

"Hey, I was listening to that," Frank said.

"I've got to stop that fool," Kelly said. "Mom, can you watch Alissa?"

"Yes, go," she said.

"Stop him? He's the answer to our prayers. Let him ride the bull, buy the ranch, and make good on his promise to be a good father," Frank said.

Kelly turned on him with tears in her eyes. "I don't want to hear one word from you about being a good father."

"Kelly," her mother said, shocked. "Now, is not the time."

"Now, is exactly the time and it should have come five years ago." She whirled back to her father and forced herself to utter the words she knew she had to say. He looked old and frail, and his natural orneriness was muted by the Johnny coat he wore. "You were wrong to throw me out of the house when I was pregnant." She turned to her mother. "And you were wrong to let him."

"Kelly," Janice said. "I agree this is a long time coming,

but not now. Not like this."

"You were wrong not to tell me who Alissa's father was," Frank countered.

"You're not helping," Janice said to her father.

Why did she think this was going to be easy? Kelly took a deep breath. "I agree."

He blinked, startled. Then he frowned and looked down at his hands. "I shouldn't have let you go to New York."

Some of the tension left her spine. This was progress.

"I'm sorry too," Sarah said. "I knew in my heart it wasn't right. But we had hoped you wouldn't go through with moving to New York. Or that you'd turn right around and come back. Had I known how long you'd stay away, I wouldn't have allowed you to go."

Kelly gave a small snort. "I don't think you could have stopped me. I inherited his temper." The apologies were good to hear. She could feel cracks in the long-held hurt that had been boarded up inside her. It didn't make anything suddenly better, but she felt it was a step in the right direction.

"All right," she said quietly. "I love Trent. I have always loved Trent. I always will love Trent. He is my daughter's father and I want to spend the rest of my life with him, if he'll have me."

"He better," Frank growled.

"Dad," she warned. "He's a good man, who is about to risk his life for us. To save your ranch. I'm going to stop him. He might get hurt really bad. What if this time, that bull puts him in a wheelchair? What if…" She choked up.

"What if it kills him? The ranch can burn down and wither for all I care. I'm going to make sure he doesn't get within ten feet of that bull. And if you can't accept that, then this is it for us."

"You giving me an ultimatum this time, little girl?" He squinted up at her with some of his usual meanness in his expression.

"You're damned right I am."

They glared at each other while Janice and her mother held their breaths.

"Fine. Stop that idiot from riding. He should have told me he wanted to breed bulls. I know a guy who…"

"I've got to go, Dad." She kissed him on the cheek and flew back out to the waiting room.

Alissa was thankfully still engrossed with her game.

"Honey, stay with Auntie Emily and MeMaw. I've got to go find Trent."

"Will he bring me another stuffie?"

"We'll see."

After hurrying down to the car, she tore out of the hospital and sped back to the Three Sisters Ranch. Trent wasn't in the studio and it was locked up tight. Why had she insisted on going back to New York City? It seemed so stupid right now. Of course, she could get an apartment in Last Stand or in a neighboring town. She could still have her Texas photo studio. The only excuse she had was that her father had tied her up in knots. And he was never going to do that again.

She would move out of the ranch house and get her own place. But it was going to be near Trent. She owed it to

Alissa—she owed it to all of them—to try to be a family.

She called his phone, but it kept ringing. No voice mail. No nothing. She got a curious case of déjà vu. Kelly called Billy King and sagged in relief when he answered.

"Billy, I need to talk to Trent."

"He can't have the distraction right now," Billy said sadly.

"I don't want him to do this. Tell him he doesn't have to ride that bull. We'll find another way. Please, Billy, please. I don't want him to get hurt."

"He ain't listening to me."

"He might listen to me. Please put him on the phone."

"He's not with me. I'm not sure where he is."

"But he will call you eventually, right? Tell him to call me."

"Kelly, I'm sorry. I don't know how to say this or if you'll even believe me. But he asked me not to tell him if you called. He said he'll call you after the event."

"When is the event going to be?"

"We're still hammering out the details, but it's going to be soon."

"Will you let me know when you find out?"

"He asked me not to tell you."

She held back a sob, by sheer force of will.

"But when I know for sure, I'll let you know," Billy said grudgingly. "I owe you."

"Thank you," Kelly whispered. It seemed like it was the day for long overdue apologies.

She drove down to the ranch house on the off chance he

was there. But he wasn't. She did see Donovan Link talking with Nate and she went over to them.

"Hey, have you guys seen Trent?" she asked.

"Yeah," Nate said. "He brought Flower over for us to look after. He's on his way to the airport."

"Airport?"

"He says he's headlining in Madison Square Garden sometime next week for a last-minute event. Do you know what that badass son of a bitch is going to do?" Nate asked.

"He's going to get himself killed," she said. "Unless, I can stop him."

Chapter Eighteen

TRENT COULD HEAR the crowd from backstage as the fans poured into the seats. He was the main event, and he had a good hour before his ride. He wanted a bottle of whiskey in the worst way. Michael was almost as excited as he was. Trent wished he was as confident in his ride as Michael was. He and Lana had backstage passes and Trent had introduced them around to the other riders and bull-fighters.

Trent had spent the last week and a half doing publicity stunts, going on talk shows and being photographed and interviewed. Corazon del Diablo was put through almost the same gauntlet. They had bull riders coming in from all over the world at the last minute to get on the ticket. It was a sold-out show.

His fucking leg ached. His hip felt scrambled from the flight and the media circus. He was chewing on Tylenol like they were Skittles.

The hardest knife ill-used doth lose its edge.

Things must be grim if he was bringing out the Shake-speare.

Now that Lana had finished up her interview with him,

he was going to head down to the arena floor in a few minutes. He wanted to drink in everything. Win or lose, Trent knew this would be his last rodeo. It felt good to have made that decision instead of having it taken from him. He could handle the pain. If he expected it, it wouldn't be too bad. More poetry lines rattled around in his head, but they flickered by too fast for him to hang on to.

"We'll see you down there," Lana said and tried to kiss him.

He turned his head and she got his cheek. She rubbed her lipstick off it with her thumb. "I wish things were different," she said.

"It is what it is."

"I guess you're right." Lana turned to go, holding Michael's hand. "But if you change your mind, let me know."

"You got it," he said.

As they left, he was expecting Billy to come in. He wasn't expecting Kelly. She launched herself into his arms and kissed him. He didn't even consider turning away. He had missed holding her. Her sweet lips and honey taste were a balm to his rioting nerves. With her here, everything clicked into place. When the intensity of the kiss got to the point that clothes were going to start coming off, he forced himself to break away and put some distance between them.

"I'm glad you're here," he said. "Where's Alissa?"

"She's with my sisters back home. Don't you ever not take my calls again."

He grinned. "Sorry."

"No, you're not."

"I needed you not to try and talk me out of this."

"Too bad, because that's what I'm here to do." She sank to her knees. "Do you want me to beg?"

"Get up." He hauled her to her feet. "Stop it." The last thing he needed was his crazy body reacting to her on her knees right now.

"You're going to get hurt and I don't want that."

He thumbed away a fat tear that coursed down her cheek. "Yeah, I'm going to get hurt. I'm going to be in agony for eight seconds. And then I'm going to be three million dollars richer. I'm going to buy the Three Sisters Ranch and build you a house on the land. It'll be yours to stay in with Alissa until you invite me to move in. And I'm giving you the deed. No one will be able to throw you out of that house. And if I don't stay on for eight seconds, I still get enough to make an offer on the ranch's mortgage. Things will take a little more time, but you and your family won't have to worry about a thing."

She took a deep, shuddering breath. "You don't have to do that. I'll stay in Last Stand. I'll stay with you, if you want. Just please don't ride that bull. It's not just going to be eight seconds of agony."

"I can't put anything past you. Yeah, I'll be in a world of hurt after tonight. But it'll be worth it." He hugged her again. "I love you."

"I love you, too. I'll do anything if you don't ride to-night."

"It's not a big deal," he lied easily.

"I wonder if Lane Frost said that."

That was dirty pool, bringing up the bull rider who'd died from his injuries. They'd made a movie about him called *8 Seconds*. Trent wasn't looking to die and he sure didn't want a movie being made about him. This was about the money, and if he was being honest with himself, it was for his ego as well.

Every man dies. Not every man really lives.

Trent hugged her tighter. "I'm not going to die. Every bullfighter in the arena is going to be concentrating on getting me clear. And I can't back out now, even if I want to—which I don't," he assured her when she looked up at him with hope in her beautiful brown eyes. "There's a sold-out arena there waiting for me."

She narrowed her eyes at him. "You're enjoying this."

"You're damned right I am. I'll let you in on a little secret." He leaned in and whispered in her ear. "I'd have done this for nothing."

"You're certifiably crazy." Kelly held on to him like she would never let go. "What am I going to do with you?"

"You're going to come down to the announcer's table and have a front-row seat. You're going to cheer me on, and then afterward, we're going to get drunk and make love all night long."

"That's pretty optimistic," she said. "What's the worst-case scenario?"

"You ride in the ambulance with me and force-feed me soup for a few weeks while my bones knit back together."

She sighed. "For better or for worse, huh? Usually you have to be married to promise to stick with someone like this."

"I'm working on it," he said. "Be patient. I need a little more time."

She punched him in the chest. "Ow." Kelly shook her hand. "Stop making fun of me."

"The vest is made to stop a bull's kick, but if you want to hit me again, go ahead by all means."

Poking him in the chest, she said, "If you get hurt, Alissa will cry."

"Now, you're playing dirty."

"I just want you to know what the stakes are."

"I know," he sighed and slid an arm around her. "I do know the stakes. But with you here, I feel like I can do anything. I love you, Kelly Sullivan."

"You better be all right. You can't say something like that and not be all right." Her voice shook.

"Of course, I'll be all right. I've got you and my daughter waiting for me." Trent kissed her as long as he dared.

"I love you, you idiot," she said, not bothering to hide her tears as she went to the announcer's table.

The grin slid off his face as he watched her walk away. This was it. The stakes were high. He needed to get his head in the arena. Trent needed to face the bull, now. Corazon del Diablo was going to let him stay on, for at least eight seconds.

Boldly they rode and well.
Into the jaws of Death.
Into the mouth of Hell.

Chapter Nineteen

KELLY WANTED TO be a coward and not watch, but she couldn't do that to Trent. And she really wanted to see that bull go down. With her nails digging half-moons into her palms, she watched the gate in tense anticipation.

The crowd must have been screaming, the music blaring, but she couldn't hear anything over the roaring in her ears. *Please. Please. Be all right.* The chemical smell of the pyrotechnics combined with fresh-popped popcorn and horse manure. Her mouth felt like she'd swallowed a bunch of pennies and her chest felt tight. This was not okay. This wasn't like the fun bull-riding events she had always looked forward to. This was way too real. Those bulls were enormous and the ground unforgiving and hard.

The gate slammed open and her heart hammered fast in panic. No. Not yet. She wasn't ready. But everyone else was. Corazon del Diablo flew out of the chute. He might be past his prime, but he wasn't a pushover. A couple of hops and a skip to the left, the bull twisted and turned in the air. Trent seesawed back and forth on top of the crazed animal. She wished she could see his face, but the helmet he wore obscured it. He was halfway through. The bull spun to the right and kicked up, nearly bucking Trent off. Throwing back his head, the bull spun in a dizzying circle, seeming to levitate before crashing down to earth.

The buzzer sounded.

Holy hell, he'd done it.

The last buck from Corazon del Diablo was a final fuck you and Trent went airborne. Hitting the ground wrong, his leg folded up under him. Corazon's back hooves missed his forehead by inches and the entire length of the bull spun over him as he continued to hop and kick. Two bullfighters were on the bull and two were on Trent. They were crowded in so tight, she couldn't see what was going on. Then, Corazon del Diablo head butted a bull rider a full ten feet across the arena. Trent was being half-dragged, half-walked out and luckily the bull didn't look twice at him.

"Come with me," Lana said, suddenly at her elbow.

Startled, Kelly hurried after her. Lana used her press pass to get them through the throngs of people. While Lana elbowed her way through, Kelly ducked and weaved until she was next to Trent's stretcher. Security was going to take her away, but Billy waved them off.

"She's with us."

"Hey," Trent said, forcing a smile even though his face was gray with pain. He reached out his hand and she clutched it with both of hers.

"You idiot," she said.

"I love you, too." He winced as the paramedics pushed the stretcher through the crowd to the waiting ambulance.

"You're going to need X-rays, but I think your hip survived the impact. That leg though…" The EMT shook his head.

Trent's face was sweaty and his breathing shallow.

"You did it," Kelly said, hoping that he hadn't injured himself permanently.

"Tell Alissa it doesn't hurt at all," he whispered.

"I will." She kissed him on the forehead.

When they lifted him into the ambulance, he cried out and then lost consciousness.

Chapter Twenty

"I SWEAR IF you don't stop trying to walk without your cane, I'm going to make you and my father share the same room," Kelly threatened, coming into his private room in the rehabilitation center. She tossed her keys on the bureau and shook her head in disgust. He wondered which nurse had tattled on him.

"Yeah," Alissa admonished. "King me." She pushed her checker to the last square on the opposite end of the board. She was sitting cross-legged on his bed, being careful not to jostle his bad side. They had set up the game on a mobile table that fit over the bed. Alissa divided her time between playing the game and reading on her tablet. The little stuffed bull he'd brought back from New York was sitting between them. The plane ride from New York to Texas had been agony, but it was worth it to be here with her. Trent would never get enough of looking at his daughter.

"Billy was telling me you've got a couple of endorsement deals in process."

"When did you talk to Billy?" Trent asked.

"This morning," she said. "He was teaching the junior class. He's bringing in some mini bulls for bucking stock next month."

Trent winced and sat up a bit. "I don't think they're ready yet."

She snorted. "I don't think you have a leg to stand on for that argument."

"Literally." He grinned.

Handing him her phone, Kelly gave him a kiss that made him wish his private room had a lock on his door. He watched the video she took of the kids and nodded. "Michael is looking good."

"Everyone sends their prayers and best wishes that you heal up quickly." Smiling, she brushed a stray hair off his forehead.

"Every day is one step closer." He was content to recuperate with his daughter and the love of his life. It beat the hell out of the last time, when it had just been him and Billy. He was fortunate and he would never take them for granted. If it took getting knocked around by that ornery bull, it was worth it.

The process of him buying the ranch from her father was a slow one that Trent was glad to let Billy and the lawyers handle. Frank was being stubborn about letting go, which shocked absolutely no one. For the moment, the ranch still belonged to the Sullivan family and might remain in the family, but Frank was willing to sell him a few acres for his school and enough for a house and a small farm. Trent had high hopes that by the time the bill of sale was finalized, no matter which way things went, he could convince Kelly to marry him.

Kelly sat at the top of the bed and took him into her arms for a kiss that made him wonder how creative they could get with his leg rebroken in three places. The doctors said he would never walk without limping. Watch him. They said he would need to use a cane for the rest of his life. They'd see about that. And they said he'd never ride a horse again.

Boy, were they in for a surprise?

He had promised Kelly, though, that his days on top of a bull were over and he would keep that promise.

"What was that for?" he asked when they came up for air.

Alissa had grown bored, waiting for him to move his checker piece and was playing a game on her mother's phone.

"Because I love you."

"I love you too," Alissa piped up.

That choked him up every time.

"And I wanted to give you a little incentive to get better soon so we can go home," she said.

"Do we have a home yet?"

"Not yet," she said. "But I think we can arrange some quality time in the Bluebonnet Inn until we have a certificate of occupancy."

"That's definitely an incentive."

They kissed until a nurse came in and cleared his throat.

"Have a good physical therapy session," Kelly said, winking at him. Her mouth was puffy from his kisses. Trent would have much rather gotten physical with her than do weight training with the nurse.

"Come on, Loverboy," the nurse said. "Let's see if you can last more than eight seconds on the rowing machine."

The End

Bibliography of Poems Trent Recites

- *"She walks in beauty, like the night." Lord Byron (George Gordon) (1788–1824).*

- *"Is this the face that launched a thousand ships and burnt the topless towers of Ilium?" Christopher Marlowe (1564–1593).*

- *"In the fell clutch of circumstance*
  I have not winced nor cried aloud.
  Under the bludgeonings of chance
  My head is bloody, but unbowed." William Ernest Henley (1849–1903).

- *"The hardest knife ill-used doth lose its edge." William Shakespeare (1564–1616).*

- *"Every man dies. Not every man really lives." William Ross Wallace (1819–1881).*

- *"Boldly they rode and well. Into the jaws of Death, into the mouth of Hell." Alfred, Lord Tennyson (1809–1892).*

If you enjoyed this book, please leave a review at your favorite online retailer! Even if it's just a sentence or two it makes all the difference.

Thanks for reading *The Cowboy's Daughter* by Jamie K. Schmidt!

Discover your next romance at TulePublishing.com.

TULE
PUBLISHING

If you enjoyed *The Cowboy's Daughter,*
you'll love the next book in....

The Three Sisters Ranch series

Book 1: *The Cowboy's Daughter*

Book 2
Coming soon!

Available now at your favorite online retailer!

About the Author

USA Today bestselling author, Jamie K. Schmidt, writes erotic contemporary love stories and paranormal romances. Her steamy, romantic comedy, Life's a Beach, reached #65 on USA Today, #2 on Barnes & Noble and #9 on Amazon and iBooks. Her Club Inferno series from Random House's Loveswept line has hit both the Amazon and Barnes & Noble top one hundred lists. The first book in the series, Heat, put her on the USA Today bestseller list for the first time, and is a #1 Amazon bestseller. Her book Stud is a 2018 Romance Writers of America Rita® Finalist in Erotica. Her dragon paranormal romance series has been called "fun and quirky" and "endearing." Partnered with New York Times bestselling author and former porn actress, Jenna Jameson, Jamie's hardcover debut, SPICE, continues Jenna's FATE trilogy.

Thank you for reading

The Cowboy's Daughter

If you enjoyed this book, you can find more from all our great authors at TulePublishing.com, or from your favorite online retailer.

Made in the USA
Middletown, DE
24 June 2020